D1525355

# You Should be My Baby

Kat Washington

You Should be My Baby

Copyright © 2017 by Kat Washington

Published by Mz. Lady P Presents

www.mzladypresents.com

This book is a work of fiction. Names, characters, places, and incidents either are the product of the author's imagination or are used fictitiously and are not to be construed as real. Any resemblance to actual persons, living or dead, business establishments, events, or locales or, is entirely coincidental.

# Table of Contents

# Chapter One: Kaya

I had been called a lot of things in my life. A prostitute, hoe, junkie, etc. But there was one thing that people couldn't call me and that was broke. I was all about my money. I believed in getting it by any means necessary. I didn't care what people thought of me, as long as I got my money, I was good. Words don't mean shit to me, but money does.

I had seen way more than I should have in my twenty years of living. Growing up, my mom didn't give two fucks about me. All she cared about was getting money and keeping it for herself. She would leave me in our small ass, rundown apartment all night while she was out doing God knows what. There would be no food for me at all, and she didn't care. My clothes were always too small, my hair was never done, and I was always hungry. I remember being excited to go to school every day just so I could eat, but that was short lived because I got made fun of because of the clothes I wore.

Our apartment was infested with roaches and rats. I could hear the rats moving around in the walls at all times of the night, and it always smelled like piss. My mom was barely there, so the smell didn't bother her. I was too afraid to leave the apartment because we lived in a terrible neighborhood. There wasn't a night that passed when I didn't hear gunshots, so I just stayed my ass right in the house.

My mom wasn't shit. Anyone with eyes could see that. She had a nice big bed in her room, while I didn't even have a room. I was stuck sleeping in the living room on the couch that she found by the dumpster. There's no telling what happened on that couch. It smelled like death, but I didn't want to sleep on the floor, so I just sucked it up and slept on the couch.

I remember my mom used to fuck niggas for money. I used to hear her loud ass on the phone bragging about it. When I was a little older, I used to listen to her conversations all the time. Niggas was really paying her to have sex with them. I thought that shit was disgusting. I remember thinking how I was going to do well in school so that I could get into a good college and make something of myself so that I wouldn't end up like my terrible mother. That was one of the things I dreamed of every night.

Too bad dreams ain't shit. Being that I didn't have anyone to discipline me, I was always in trouble. When I got to high school, bitches were always trying me and talking shit because I couldn't afford cute clothes and shit. I wasn't having that shit, though. Fighting had become an everyday thing for me and I guess the principal got tired of talking to me because she eventually expelled me.

I was sixteen when I got kicked out of school and I didn't know what to do. I didn't want to tell my mom because I knew she would probably put her hands on me that day. I don't think she could beat my ass or anything, but she was still my mom and I didn't want to fight her. I knew that she was going to wonder why I was at home in the morning, so I got my things ready and left out of the apartment like I was going to school, even though I wasn't.

What should I do now? I was sixteen years old and I was kicked out of school. Should I start looking for a job? What if no one would hire me? Then what? I was so mad at myself for getting kicked out of school. I was walking down the street when I saw a boy that looked to be a couple of years older than me, robbing some old ass man. He took everything that the old man had and was about to take off running before he saw me standing there, staring at him. He took off running and being the dumb ass that I am, I followed him.

He didn't like the fact that I was following him, so he turned around and aimed a gun at my head. Most sixteen-year-old girls would've probably been scared or ran away, or maybe even begged that nigga not to pull the trigger, but I wasn't like most sixteen-year-old girls. I simply looked at that nigga in his eyes and said, "Shoot me." I didn't care about life anyway. I didn't have anyone that cared about me so I figured why not just die? Wouldn't that be the easy way out? Of course he didn't shoot me, though. He was shocked that I wasn't afraid of him or his gun.

And that's when it all started. He told me his name was Kevin and he was nineteen. I started to chill with him a lot. Eventually, I started robbing niggas with him. He showed me how to do it, and after I robbed the first man, I wanted more. Not only were we mugging people on the streets, but we were kicking in doors, stealing and selling everything that we could. I was making money and I was happy as hell.

My mom found out that I had gotten kicked out of school, so she kicked me out of her apartment. I wasn't pregnant, I wasn't sneaking boys into the house, I wasn't disrespectful, yet she still felt the need to put a sixteen-year-old out on the streets. I didn't argue with her or anything. I knew exactly where I could go.

Kevin had become like a big brother to me. He was very overprotective when it came to me and I liked that a lot. I never really had anyone care for me the way Kevin did. Eventually, I started telling people that he was my older brother. He would always tell me that blood didn't make you related, but loyalty does. He had been loyal to me ever since I was sixteen.

"So what you got going on later?" this dude named Greg asked as I put my clothes back on. He was one of the dudes I was fucking because he was giving me money. Yeah, I know I said that I would never be like my mom, but I guess the apple doesn't fall too far from the tree.

"I don't know. I'm working tonight, though," I let him know.

"You don't need to be in that club working anyway. I told you that I got you." It took everything in me not to roll my eyes at his ass. Greg wasn't nothing but a corner boy.

4

What the hell could I do with that? I was making more money than him by robbing niggas, stripping, and taking money from the niggas who willingly give it up. This nigga barely had himself.

"Greg, what about your girlfriend? Why don't you tell her to quit her job so that you can take care of her?" I asked, looking at him with an eyebrow raised. I knew all about his girlfriend, Amaya. I mean, it wasn't like he tried to hide it from me or anything. She wasn't anything but a hoe. She was fucking my brother because I saw her leaving the house early in the morning plenty of times. She worked at some store in the mall. Couldn't be me because I wasn't down with someone telling me what to do and when to do it. Not at all.

"I need to make sure she's the one for me before I tell her to do all that," he said, firing up a blunt. This nigga was stupid as hell. He had to make sure she was the one, but he was telling me to quit what I do to make money? Yeah, that's not about to happen.

"And you think I'm the one for you? When you got a whole girlfriend?"

"Hell yeah." I shook my head at his goofy ass. I wasn't about to entertain him. It was always the same thing with him. He wanted me all to himself and that wasn't going to happen anytime soon. Especially not with him. This nigga couldn't stay faithful if his life depended on it, and I would have to kill his ass. I'm not good with sharing.

Greg wasn't an ugly dude at all. He kept a low cut and his waves were nice as hell. He was light skin with a few tattoos. He wasn't as tall as I'd prefer, but he was taller than me, so that was good enough for me. He had a six pack, but he was still skinny as hell. You could tell that he didn't play sports when he was in high school. I didn't like that at all. Greg wasn't my type. I couldn't deal with a nigga like him.

"Alright, I'm about to go. I'll hit you up later," I told him, holding my hand out. He looked at me, but he knew what was up. He reached over to his dresser, then put a stack of money in my hand. I was all smiles as I left his condo. Money was the one thing that made me happy, not these niggas. I only needed a nigga for one thing and that was dick. Other than that, they can keep that relationship stuff to themselves.

I got in my black 2015 Mercedes Benz and was on the way to the house that I shared with my brother. I kind of wanted my own place, but at the same time, I enjoyed living with him. He was always giving me money too. He didn't agree with me stripping, but he knew there was nothing he could say to change my mind because I was all about my money.

Pulling into the driveway of our house, I put the money that I had gotten from Greg in my purse, then I stepped out of the car. I was probably going to go chill with my best friend, Clay, later, but first I had to take a shower. I felt dirty and I wasn't going anywhere feeling like this.

Walking through the front door, the place was a mess. There were clothes all over the place. Not my clothes, but Kevin's clothes. I then heard yelling coming from upstairs, so I knew it had to be one of Kevin's bitches that were tripping today. I rolled my eyes because I really wasn't in the mood to deal with this shit right now.

I slowly made my way up the stairs and into Kevin's room. For some reason, his females always thought they meant more to him than just some free pussy. He was always arguing with someone and it was annoying. I always had to be the peace maker in these situations because if not, my brother might end up in jail. He was a hot head at times and he would kill a bitch with his bare hands. I watched him do it before. It wasn't a pleasant thing to see either.

"I'm so sick of you treating me like I'm just some hoe, Kevin!" I heard a voice that I knew all too well. Why the hell was this bitch even here? I stepped into Kevin's room to see him sitting on the edge of the bed, scrolling through his phone, not looking like he cared about what Amaya was saying to him at all.

"You are a hoe," Kevin said without even looking up at her. I snickered and she turned to look at me.

"Are you fucking her too? Is she who you were just on the phone with? I know she's not your real sister. Y'all don't even look alike!" Amaya yelled.

"Bitch, she is my fucking sister. You need to go clean up the mess you made downstairs, then get the fuck out. I'm tired of hearing your annoying ass voice," Kevin said. I was shocked that Kevin hadn't already put his hands on her for fucking with his clothes. That's one thing that he didn't play about.

"I'm not going nowhere!" she yelled, slapping his phone out of his hand. Kevin stood up and wrapped his hand around her neck. I saw it coming. She was doing too much anyway. Some people can't take rejection, I see.

"Bitch, I told you to stop fucking acting like I'm your motherfucking boyfriend and won't kill your ass right here!" Amaya was clawing at his hands, so I quickly went to intervene.

"Kevin, chill out. Don't kill this bitch in here. Let her go," I said, standing in front of him. He looked at me, then back at her. He threw her down on the ground and she started coughing and gasping for air.

"Get this bitch away from me, bruh," Kevin said, then he walked off into his bathroom and slammed his door. I helped Amaya off of the floor and she snatched away from me.

"Don't fucking touch me, bitch!" she yelled. She was obviously feeling herself right now and she clearly didn't know where my hands were.

"Look, Amaya, you need to take your ass on before you end up hurt. I'm trying to be nice about it, but you're making it really hard." She looked at me with narrow eyes.

"How the hell do you know my name?" she asked.

*Because I'm fucking your boyfriend, stupid bitch*, I thought to myself.

"Don't worry about all that. You just need to leave." She folded her arms across her chest.

"I'm not going anywhere. Kevin needs to learn some respect and stop treating me like a hoe." I was really getting tired of this bitch. Why wouldn't she just leave? Why was she making everything so difficult?

"Amaya, let's be real. You are fucking my brother while you're in another relationship. That is definitely considered a hoe. Now please get the fuck out. I got shit to do and you're cutting into that." I was trying to be nice to the girl, but she was making me want to drag her by her hair and put her out.

"I am not in a relationship," she lied. I chuckled.

"Okay. I'll let Greg know you said that the next time he calls me for some pussy." Her eyes grew wide as hell. I guess she thought Greg was faithful. Silly girl.

"You're lying. Greg doesn't call you. He wouldn't even mess with someone like you."

"Right. Don't be mad, baby girl. Your nigga gives me money every time we fuck. What has he given you? Not a damn thing. Now get the fuck out. I'm not going to tell you no more." I was getting tired of repeating myself.

"You're pathetic. You're really sitting here making up stories, for what? You know damn well you don't know Greg," she said and started laughing. I wasn't going to say anything, but she was really starting to piss me off. I reached into my purse and grabbed my cell phone. I dialed Greg's number and put him on speaker. He answered on the second ring.

"Damn, Kaya. You missing the dick already?" he asked. I laughed lightly because Amaya's face was priceless.

"Boy, you crazy. Did I leave my diamond necklace over there? I can't seem to find it," I said, knowing damn well my necklace was around my neck.

"Nah, I don't see it. Don't stress it, though. I'll buy you another one," he said.

"Okay. I'll call you later." I ended the call and looked at Amaya. She looked like she wanted to cry.

"Now can you please leave?" I said, obviously annoyed.

"You ain't shit but a prostitute! Nasty ass bitch!" she yelled. I was over it. I put my purse and cell phone down and sent a punch straight to her jaw. She stumbled back and fell on the floor. I grabbed her by her hair and drug her to the top of the stairs. I let her hair go because she was kicking and screaming, but then I kicked her stupid ass down the stairs.

After that, I made my way down the stairs right behind her and grabbed her by her hair again and threw her out of the house. I was so tired of this bitch. I didn't know why the hell she couldn't just leave to begin with. Why the hell was she making it so hard?

I walked back in the house, then went straight to my room. I was tired now. I didn't even feel like going anywhere.

I got in my bed and laid down. Before I knew it, I had drifted off to sleep.

# Chapter Two: Kevin

I guess I was going to have to stop fucking with Amaya. That bitch was really crazy. She started trippin' after my phone rang and I answered it. Shit, it was Katrina. Another one of the bitches I fucked daily. Why wouldn't I answer it? Amaya was supposed to be on her way out anyway. I was tired of her. All I wanted to do was get my dick sucked and send her on her way. She had to make shit difficult, though.

I finished up my shower and came out of the bathroom. Amaya had taken my clothes and threw them all over the place. I should go find her stupid ass so I could put a bullet in her damn head. She had me so fucked up. I was really done fucking with her. There was no way around it. I put on some clothes and went to go check on Kaya. I had to make sure she didn't try to kill Amaya too. She always spoke about my bad temper, when hers was just as bad as mine, if not worse.

Kaya was knocked out on her bed. I was used to that, though. She would be out all night and then come home and sleep all day. Then do the same thing all over again the next day. I didn't know how she did it. I kissed her on her forehead and then I left the house. I decided that I was going to go see what my niggas were up to since I didn't want to be in the house bored as hell.

About fifteen minutes later, I pulled up to the tattoo shop that the homie Rome owned. I swear this nigga was here more than he was at home. I didn't blame him, though. He was making money, the legal way. I'm pretty sure his girl didn't like him being gone all day, though. You know how females can get—always complaining about some shit.

I parked the car and got out. Walking into the building, I looked right at the receptionist. She rolled her eyes at me and tried to act like she was busy. I chuckled to myself and decided that I was going to fuck with her.

"What's good, Brandi? Why you rolling your eyes at a nigga?" I asked.

"Kevin, get the fuck out my face. I'm trying to work and you're over here distracting me," she said with an attitude. I didn't know why the hell she had an attitude; I didn't do shit to her ass.

"You ain't doing shit but straightening papers that are already straightened. Why you got an attitude with me? What I do to you?" She looked at me like she wanted to punch me in the face.

"You know exactly what you did. How you gonna fuck me for two days straight, then when I leave, I don't get a text message, a phone call or anything? You wouldn't even return any of my calls! You treated me like I was just some hoe." I could tell she was obviously still feeling some type of way about it, but she knew how I was when she begged to suck my dick. Yeah, I treated her like she was a hoe because that's

14

exactly what she was to me. That's what all the bitches I fucked with were to me.

"You knew what it was when you started fucking with me. You heard all of the stories because you were telling me about them, so there's no need to act shocked when it happens to you." She was quiet for a minute. She looked like she was in deep thought.

Brandi was pretty as hell. She had long jet black hair that stopped in the middle of her back, her stomach was flat and toned, and her thighs were thick as hell. Usually how I liked my women. She didn't have the biggest ass, but she had enough back there for me to grab on while I was hitting it from the back. Her almond skin was smooth and there wasn't a mole or blemish in sight. She was definitely the model type. She just wasn't my type. She sucked my dick right here in the bathroom of Rome's shop. We hadn't even known each other for a good hour. Now, what nigga would want to wife a female like her? She made herself too available.

"Kevin, are you even listening to me?" Brandi asked, bringing me out of my thoughts.

"Naw, I wasn't really. You should come through later, though," I said. I didn't give a fuck about none of the shit she was saying. I was now thinking about how her lips felt wrapped around my dick and now I felt myself getting hard. She looked at me like I was crazy.

"What? You really want me to come over so that you can fuck my brains out then act like you never met me?" She chuckled like something was funny. That's exactly what I had planned to do to her. I was glad that she knew.

"It was a yes or no question. I didn't need to hear all of that extra shit that you just said to me."

"Why don't you call up one of your many bitches? I know you got hoes waiting in line to fuck you." She was obviously salty as hell that I wasn't trying to fuck with her how she was trying to fuck with me. I didn't care, though.

"You right. I don't even know why I'm over here still wasting my breath with you," I said and I started to walk off.

"Wait," I heard her call from behind me. I turned around to look at her. "I get off at eight. What time do you want me to come over?"

"I'll call you when I'm ready for you," I said, then walked to the back where Rome was. I could've taken Brandi into the bathroom right now, but I wasn't feeling it. Plus, I was drained from fucking with Amaya earlier.

"What's good niggas?" I asked as I walked into the little office Rome had in his shop. He was sitting on the couch drinking a beer with that nigga Royal right beside him. I dapped both of them up, then took a seat on the other couch that was across from them.

"I was wondering when your slow ass was going to show up. You ready to work for a nigga yet?" Rome asked. He wanted me to be one of the tattoo artist in his shop, but I wasn't feeling that shit. Yeah, I could draw my ass off and shit, but I didn't see myself putting tattoos on people's skin.

"I don't know how many times I gotta tell your goofy ass no," I said, getting up to get me a beer out of the mini-fridge.

"I could make a lot more money if you were to come." I understood all of that, but robbing niggas, robbing houses, and occasionally selling dope was good enough for me right now. I was making a decent amount of money to take care of me and my little sister.

"Yeah, I feel you on that, but I'm making good enough money right now," I said.

"Good enough? Hell nah, nigga. Ain't no such thing as good enough money. You should get further into the game with me. I'm working on getting my own product and flooding the streets of Atlanta. I'd be working for myself and shit," Royal said. He was deep into the drug game. I don't think he had any plans of quitting and going legit either.

"You really want to be robbing niggas for the rest of your life?" Rome asked. It's not something that I planned on doing for the rest of my life. I wanted to open up a couple of barber shops and car washes. I thought about opening up a strip club, but I wasn't feeling that shit. Knowing my ass, I would probably end up fucking about half of the strippers that worked for me and that would start a lot of unnecessary drama that I wasn't trying to deal with.

"No, I don't want to be robbing niggas for the rest of my life, but right now, that's what's putting food on the table. I do want to open up some barbershops and car washes, though. Start making money the legal way." They both just nodded their heads, letting me know that they understood what I was saying.

"How's that fine ass sister of yours?" Rome asked me. He was always asking about Kaya, but he was with her best friend, Clay.

"She's good and not worried about your ass," I let him know.

"Nigga, you got a sister? She single?" Royal asked. This nigga had known me for years now and still didn't know that I had a sister. That shows how much attention he pays to other people's lives.

"Yeah, I got a sister. But as for that single shit, I don't know what she does with her life," I said being honest. I knew Kaya had niggas that she fucked with, but I never got involved with any of that. What she does is her business so I just let her be. As long as she doesn't come to me telling me that one of these nigga's put their hands on her, then I'm good.

"I might have to meet her. See what's up with that." I ignored what Royal said. Knowing Kaya, she probably wouldn't give him the time of day. She wasn't very fond of cocky niggas. I wasn't going to tell him that because he would probably think that I was just trying to stop him from pursuing my sister, and I couldn't care less about that.

I stayed at the shop for a couple of hours chilling with these niggas. I didn't realize what time it was until I looked down at my phone. I decided to take my ass home and wait for Brandi to get off so she could come through. I hope she didn't change her mind. It wouldn't really make a difference though because I had plenty of bitches just waiting for me to call their asses.

As I was walking out of the shop, I locked eyes with Brandi. She looked like she was beyond ready to get off so that I could be up in her guts. I was feeling the same way she was.

"Bye, Kevin. I'll call you as soon as I get off," she said and smiled at me. I nodded my head and kept it moving to my car. As soon as I got in the driver's seat, my phone started ringing. I looked at the screen and saw that it was Amaya calling me. This bitch just didn't get the hint. I hit ignore and started up my car. She called right back, so this time, I answered.

"What?" I asked.

"Why would you let that bitch attack me like that?" she sobbed into the phone. I really wasn't in the mood for this right now.

"Fuck you talkin' about?"

"Your sister! She put her hands on me! I got a black eye because of her!" I chuckled thinking about Kaya beating Amaya's ass. I didn't know what the fuck had happened once I went into the bathroom. I heard some screaming, but I figured that Kaya had it under control.

"That ain't my fault. Learn how to fight," I said nonchalantly.

"Why do you treat me like this? Why can't you love me as much as I love you?" I just laughed at her stupid ass.

"Because love don't live here." I ended the call before she could even respond back to me. Truth is, I don't think I knew how to love anyone other than myself and my sister. I wasn't shown love growing up, so I didn't know how to do it, really.

I grew up in a foster home. I never met my mom or dad. I never got adopted because I was a troubled child growing up. I basically did what I wanted and I didn't do too well with other people telling me what to do. So, I did my own thing.

I was always getting into fights and shit because niggas would try me thinking that I was just going to sit around and let them punk my ass. That's probably the reason my ass never got adopted. By the time I was eighteen, I had aged out. I didn't have a job, a place to live, or a way to eat. I had a couple of friends that were small-time hustlers, but I wasn't feeling that. I didn't want to work for anyone but myself, so I did what I had to do to start making fast money, which was robbing niggas. It was easy to do, especially in those rich ass neighborhoods. Most of those white people didn't even expect it to happen.

I guess they thought that since they lived in one of those high-class neighborhoods, they were safe. They were sadly mistaken, though. Those are the neighborhoods that Kaya and I robbed the most. A lot of them didn't even have alarm systems in their house and that made it even easier. It was amazing how stupid rich people were.

When I made it home, Kaya was awake and all of the clothes from downstairs were cleaned up. I knew that was Kaya's doing. She was a neat freak and she couldn't stand anything being a mess. I told her that we could easily hire a maid, but she wasn't feeling that shit at all. She said it's not that hard to clean up and that I should try it one day. Why should I if she cleans up before a mess is even made?

"Nigga, you need to learn how to control your bitches," Kaya said once I made it to the top of the stairs.

"I do control them." I smiled, knowing damn well that was a lie.

"I'm tired of cleaning up after y'all all of the time. Either you're going to start controlling them, or you need to start taking them bitches to a hotel or some shit." She rolled her eyes at me and made her way back into her room. She was wearing a short ass nude dress and her hair was in hair rollers. I knew she was getting ready for work, so I went into my room and laid out on the bed. I guess I would just chill right here until it was time for Brandi to get off.

# Chapter Three: Royal

After that nigga Kevin left, it was just Rome and I chillin' in his office. I didn't really have shit to do tonight, so I was probably just gonna take my ass home and order pizza or some shit. It was nights like this when I wished I had a woman to come home to. I got lonely as hell at night.

Rome blew out a frustrated breath and sat his phone down on the desk. From the looks of it, he was probably going through it with his girl. They were always having problems. They weren't even married yet, but they argued like they were. He gave her a ring, but I didn't see how they were going to get married. It seemed like all they did was argue. Every time I saw those two together, they were arguing. Every time she called his phone, they were arguing. Maybe it's just me, but I don't like a bitch that likes to argue. I didn't know how Rome put up with it. I would've been stopped fucking with that girl.

"You good over there? You look like you're stressing," I said, walking to the mini-fridge and getting me another beer.

"Nah, Clay trippin' on my ass again," he said, shaking his head. I already knew that, though.

"Why she trippin' now?"

"Same shit. She thinks I'm out with another bitch and not working. I fucked up a couple of times and she won't let it go. She doesn't trust my ass at all anymore."

"I don't need those types of problems. That's why I stay single," I told him, turning up my beer.

"You'll find a girl one day. And when you do, you're going to do every single thing she asks you to do. No matter how stupid that shit is. The other day, she had me out buying tampons for her ass. Do you know how many brands and sizes tampons come in?" I chuckled.

"Nigga, you actually bought tampons for that girl? What was wrong with her legs and car?"

"She wasn't feeling good. I wasn't about to send her out knowing she felt shitty. That's fucked up. And plus, I love that girl. I try my hardest to keep her happy." This girl had really turned my nigga soft. He used to be like me. Fuck a bitch one day and not even think about her the next day. That's what he was supposed to do with Clay, but I don't know what happened. She must've had gold between her legs or some shit.

"I don't care how much I'm feeling a bitch. You will not catch me out buying tampons and shit. Got me fucked up," I said.

"Yeah, you say that shit now, but just wait on it. You're going to find your match one day and she's going to have your head gone." I waved him off because I was sure that wasn't going to happen anytime soon. I wasn't looking for a relationship with no bitch. They were only good for one thing and that was pussy.

I was tired of going home by myself every night, but I still wasn't looking for a relationship. All I was worried about was making money. Maybe after I got to where I wanted to be in life with my money, I would try settling down. But right now, I was good on that.

"I doubt that will ever happen," I told Rome. He just shook his head and laughed at me like he knew some shit. Just because he was pussy whipped doesn't mean that was going to ever happen to me. I knew how to control myself and my feelings.

"Whatever you say, bruh. What you on tonight, though?"

"Shit. I didn't have any plans. I was about to take my ass home and order some pizza or some shit," I shrugged.

"Nigga, that's what you do every night. That shit sounds lonely as hell since you don't allow anyone to come over to your crib."

"Nigga, fuck you. I'm good. Plus, I don't want everyone knowing where I stay at. You never know what could happen."

"Let's hit up the strip club tonight. I haven't been in a minute, plus I'm not ready to go home to Clay yet. I want to at least have a little bit of fun before I have to go home and deal with her."

"Shit, I'm down. I'm just gonna go change and I'll meet you there," I said, standing up and holding my hand out so that he could dap me up.

"Aight. Don't take all day either. You know you get ready slower than a bitch." I flipped him off and walked out of the shop. As always, all eyes were on me. That happened everywhere I went, though. Bitches couldn't help but stare at my good looking ass. Even when they were with their niggas. It wasn't my fault that they couldn't control their bitches, though.

I didn't even care to get all dressed up like I usually do. All of the attention was going to be on Rome and me as soon as we stepped into the building anyway. Plus, it didn't matter what I was wearing; I could leave the club with any bitch I wanted.

I met Rome back when I was a sophomore in high school. He was quiet and didn't really talk much and I had to be his partner one day in science class. I noticed that he stayed with all the new clothes and shoes. He never looked like he was a thrown away child and bitches flocked to his ass. They would look at me and keep it moving because of the old clothes and shoes that I was still wearing. I wanted to be on Rome's level and I also wanted to help my mom out since I didn't have a dad. So, I approached that nigga and asked if he had a job.

He told me that he was in the drug game and told me exactly what I needed to do to get put on. That's not what I had in mind, but anything was better than watching my mom struggle and wearing clothes that were beginning to become too small for me to fit. Right now, I was down for whatever.

I wasn't the wealthiest growing up. My mom was working as a nurse to provide for me and her. She had lost her job and it was hard for her to find another one, so we started struggling.

My mom used to stay up for hours calling around, trying her hardest to find another job because she needed a way to feed her only child. I hated seeing my mom like that. She used to wake me up in the middle of the night because I could hear her loud cries. No one wants to see their mom struggle. I felt less of a man, even though I was only sixteen.

The money started rolling in faster than I expected it to. At first, all I was selling was weed and I thought I was bringing home a decent amount of money. But Rome introduced me to selling dope and it was over from there. I moved my mom out of our rundown apartment in the hood and into a nice two-story house in the suburbs. Of course, she didn't like the idea of me selling drugs to make money, but she had no choice but to deal with it. She still didn't have a job and I was bringing in the only income. I'm still taking care of her to this day. She enjoys not working. I've been cool with Rome ever since because he basically looked out for a nigga.

I decided to just wear a red Polo tee, with some black denim jeans. I paired it with a pair of black and red Jordans and put my dreads in a low ponytail. I put on a gold chain, then I was out of the door. I wasn't feeling the club tonight, but I was going to take my ass anyway. It was better than sitting in the house for the rest of the night.

Pulling up to the club, it was packed as hell. That was expected, though. Bitches stayed trying to get into the strip club because they knew niggas with money would be there. All they were looking for was a come up. That's another reason I wasn't pressed to be in a relationship. Bitches see a nigga like me and all they see are dollar signs. I wasn't about to be anyone's meal ticket.

I parked my car and walked up to the front of the line. Being that my name rang bells in the streets, I didn't have to wait in line for shit.

"Hey, Royal!" a few of the girls standing in line called out to me. I just threw my hand up and kept it moving. I probably didn't even know who these hoes were. But then again, I might have fucked a couple of them and just forgot.

As soon as I stepped into the club, I spotted Rome in the VIP section with a couple of bitches dancing all over his lap. He must've been drunk as hell because most of the time, he won't even let another female touch him. I was about to make my way up to his section, but I spotted one of the dancers walking towards the bar. She outshined every other stripper in here and it looked like she didn't even try very hard to do so.

She had almond brown skin with long jet black weave that stopped right above her ass. Her boobs were looking real nice in the little top she had on and her ass looked like she could've paid for it. But I could tell that it was all natural. That G-string that she had on didn't stand a chance. I wanted to take her home with me tonight. She was looking way too good to go home by herself.

I walked over to the bar so that I could talk to her. Her back was turned to me and I really just wanted to bend her ass over right here, but there were way too many people in here that would be watching. I watched as she downed three shots back to back, then asked for another round.

"Damn ma, don't you think you need to slow down?" I asked. She turned and looked at me, but she didn't look impressed with me at all. That was a first.

"Don't you think you need to back up?" she spat and rolled her eyes.

"Nah, I don't think you want me to do that," I said, inching closer to her.

"Nigga, I didn't even want you to come over here bothering me. Now, what makes you think that I would want you to be here in my personal space while I'm trying to get drunk?" I didn't think she knew who I was. Otherwise, she wouldn't be talking to me like I was just some random ass nigga on the streets.

"Damn, why you gotta treat a nigga like that, though?" I chuckled.

"Niggas like you approach me all night, every night. I'm sorry that I'm not feeling it. Now like I said, I'm trying to get drunk so you can go prey on the next stripper," she said, dismissing me. I chuckled again.

"So what's your name?" I asked, sitting down on the stool beside her.

"Not interested." She rolled her eyes.

"Alright, Miss Not Interested. Can I get your number or something? You're too beautiful for me not to call you tonight." She looked at me and burst out laughing like I had told the funniest joke.

"I'm good, my nigga. All you want to do is take me to a hotel, fuck me, and then act like we never met. I'm not stupid. I know exactly what your motives are. Who comes to a strip club looking for a wife? Nobody. So like I said, you can run along and find you a different stripper. I'm here to make money and nothing else." She finished her last shot, then stood up and walked away. I watched her ass the whole time she made her way back into the crowd.

I just sat at the bar in a daze. I couldn't believe that she had handled my ass like that. Any other time, I would've just said fuck that bitch and kept it moving, but something was different about her. She wasn't like all of these other thirsty ass bitches in here. She was all about her money and I could see that just from that one conversation.

I had to have her in my life. I didn't know what it was about her, but I wanted to be able to say that I was fucking her. She was something to brag about for real. I didn't even get her name. I was sure that I was going to run into her again, though. And when I did, I was going to have her ass bent over, screaming my name. I couldn't wait either.

# Chapter Four: Rome

All I was trying to do was have a good time with my boy Royal before I had to go home and deal with Clay's mouth and her accusations. I probably shouldn't have gone to the strip club, but I haven't been in like a month. I felt like I deserved it. All I did was work and come home to Clay. That shit got boring. I knew I could've asked Clay to come with me to the strip club, but she has a problem when other girls stare at me. Clay wasn't a scary chick at all, so she would always say something. That was just drama that I didn't want to deal with.

I was sitting on the couch in VIP with this sexy ass stripper sitting on my lap. I admit that I shouldn't have been doing this, but I was drunk and high. I wasn't thinking straight at all. I was just glad to be out and enjoying myself. I looked over at Royal and he looked like he was enjoying himself too. I mean, who wouldn't be? We're in a club full of half-naked bitches. That would make any man happy. Unless that nigga is gay or some shit.

"This is how you work, Romeo?!" I heard Clay's voice yell. I didn't tell her that I planned on going out and I wasn't replying to any of her messages. Then on top of all that, I still had this bitch sitting on my lap.

I looked at Clay standing in front of me with her hands folded across her chest and her friend Kaya standing right next to her, giving me a stank ass look. I forgot that Kaya worked at this club. I should've went to a different one. Shit.

"Clay—" I started to say, but she cut me off by pulling the girl on my lap onto the floor by her hair. I should've known this was going to happen. I should've told ole girl to get off of me when she first sat down, but I wasn't thinking at all.

"This is why we're having problems now! You're a fucking liar!" she yelled at me. She slapped me hard as hell and I bit my bottom lip to keep my temper under control.

"Don't bother bringing your ass home! Stay here with this bitch since she's important enough to sit on your lap!" Clay yelled and walked out of our section. Kaya started to follow her, but I grabbed her arm. If looks could kill, I would be a dead ass nigga.

"Kaya, why you do me like that?" I asked, referring to Clay. She rolled her eyes at me and snatched her arm away from me.

"Because, you ain't shit, nigga! How would you feel if Clay was up in a club, sitting on another nigga's lap? You would kill him and her, so I don't want to hear anything you need to say. Clay has been nothing but good to your ass and you keep shitting on her. Maybe this time, she'll leave your dog ass for good!" she yelled. The thought of Clay leaving me for good had me feeling some type of way. I didn't want to lose her at all.

"So your name is Kaya?" Royal asked her. She rolled her eyes again.

"I'm still not interested, nigga," she said, then walked out of our section. Royal was looking like he wanted to run after Kaya and give her his all. I wanted to ask what that was about, but I had to go make things right with my girl.

"I'll get up with you later. I gotta go make sure Clay isn't about to leave my ass," I told Royal.

"Pussy whipped ass nigga," he chuckled.

"Fuck you. You're next," I said, pointing to Kaya. He waved me off and I left the club. Knowing Clay, she was probably packing her shit and was about to go to her mother's house. That's what she always did when we were having relationship problems. I hated that shit because her mom was always up in our business. She would act like Clay wasn't a grown ass woman and couldn't handle her own. I hated that shit so much.

Pulling up to the crib Clay and I shared, I was shocked to see her car parked in the driveway. I just knew that she wouldn't have even come home. I was glad she was home though. I needed to let her know that she was the only woman for me, even though I keep fucking up.

The smell of bleach slapped me in the face as soon as I walked through the front door. I didn't see Clay downstairs, so I knew she was upstairs in the bathroom. I was hoping like hell she wasn't bleaching my clothes and was just cleaning the house, but with everything that was going on right now, I already knew what was going on.

I ran into the bathroom to see Clay sitting on the toilet, crying her eyes out with half of my wardrobe in the bathtub with bleach all over it. I didn't know what to do. I wanted to wring Clay's neck for fucking up my clothes, but at the same time, I wanted to hold her until she stopped crying. I didn't want to see her upset, especially over something that I had caused.

"Clay," I said. She finally looked up at me, then rolled her eyes.

"Just leave. I don't want you here," she said.

"You don't mean that."

"I do. I'm tired of being the one that always leaves, so you just go. I don't want anything else to do with you. You don't love me. I've done nothing but love you unconditionally, and I can't even get the same in return. Go back to the strip club. I could tell you were having a lot of fun there," she said.

"Well, at least the strippers don't nag me all of the damn time." She looked up at me with so much hatred in her eyes. I knew I had fucked up even more.

"You want to know why they don't nag you all the time? Because you're not engaged to them. They don't have to worry about you cheating on them because all they want is your money. They didn't walk in on you fucking another bitch in the house that we share. They didn't have to deal with females laughing at them because their nigga couldn't keep his dick in his pants." Clay shook her head and stood up off of the toilet.

"You know what, this isn't even worth it anymore," she said, walking into our bedroom.

"What are you talking about? What's not worth it?" I asked, dreading the answer.

"This relationship! It's obvious that other females are more important than me. So, I'll let you just be single. It's for the best," she said, walking into the closet and grabbing clothes.

"Those bitches don't mean shit to me, Clay! At the end of the day, you're the one with the ring!" I yelled.

"That ring doesn't mean shit if you're still out acting single! Why the hell would I want to be with a man like that?!"

"I'm not out here acting single! I come home to you every night! I talk to you all damn day while I'm trying to work! What more do you want from me?" She stared at me for a minute before she slid her ring off of her finger and handed it to me.

"I want you to just leave me alone," she said with her voice cracking. She continued to grab her things and put them in a duffel bag. She wasn't leaving me. She really had me fucked up if she thought that I was going to just let her walk out of my life like this.

I grabbed her duffel bag and threw it to the other side of the room. Before she could even say anything, I pushed her down onto the bed and got on top of her.

"Rome, get off of me. I'm serious," she said, looking me in my eyes.

"No," I said and started kissing her on her neck.

"Stop it." Her mouth was saying one thing, but I could tell by her body language that she didn't want me to stop.

I quickly removed her shirt and she wasn't wearing a bra underneath. It's not like she needed to wear one anyway. She had a perfect set of perky breasts. They weren't too big and they weren't too small either. I took one of her hard nipples into my mouth and she didn't even try to stop me. She knew she wasn't going anywhere. She just had to cause a scene, like always.

"Romeee," she moaned. I felt myself about to bust out of my pants, so I quickly removed the pants that she was wearing, then stepped out of mine. She was watching me the whole time with an attitude.

"Spread them," I said, coming closer to her.

"No. You don't even have on a condom," she said. I didn't care about any of that though. If she got pregnant, then that would be just fine with me. I wanted to start a family with her anyway.

"I'm good," I told her as I spread her legs apart.

"You better pull out, Rome!" I ignored her as I slid all ten inches inside of her. Why would I put on a condom when she felt this damn good? I usually only put on condoms because she wants me to, but I was done with that.

"Romeee, wait!" she yelled, but I couldn't. She was feeling way too good for me to stop or slow down. It was probably the alcohol that had me feeling like this, because most of the time, I would be extra gentle with her.

"Shit," I said under my breath. I looked down at her and she had her eyes closed with her mouth hanging open. Her moans were like music to my ears. I pulled out and flipped her over onto her stomach. I knew it was about to be over because this position always got my ass.

"ROMEO, I'M GONNA CUMMM!" she yelled. I grabbed a handful of her hair as she coated my dick with her juices.

"Are you still leaving me?" I asked, forcefully pumping in and out of her.

"Nooo…Daddy…I'm not leaving!"

"Yo' ass gonna put that ring back on?"

"YESS!" I felt myself about to cum, so I started going even harder. She was screaming loud as hell and I was glad that the neighbors couldn't hear us. Someone would probably call 911 on us because they thought I was killing her.

"Fuckkk!" I yelled as I came long and hard inside of her.

"Rome! I told you to pull out!" she yelled, as I pulled out of her and fell over on the bed.

"Girl, be quiet. You act like having my baby is such a bad thing," I said with my eyes closed. She didn't say anything else. I felt her get off the bed, then she slammed the door once she was in the bathroom. She could have an attitude all she wanted. As long as she wasn't leaving me, I was good.

I woke up the next morning in bed by myself. That was odd because Clay always woke me up with breakfast. I looked at the clock and it was almost twelve in the afternoon. This shit wasn't normal at all.

I got out of bed and made my way downstairs where I heard talking coming from in the kitchen. It was Clay's voice, but it sounded like she was trying to whisper. I didn't smell any food being cooked either. She had her back to me, so she didn't even know that I was behind her.

"I just got back home from getting it. Do I take it now or should I wait?" she said to whoever was on the other side of the call.

"I'm scared, what if Rome finds out?" After she said that, I didn't even want to listen anymore. I needed to know who she was talking about and who she was talking to.

"What if I find out what?" I asked, causing her to jump. She turned around and looked at me, then quickly ended her call.

"Nothing," she quickly said.

"Who the hell were you talking to? And what's in that bag?" I asked, noticing that she was holding a bag from Walgreens.

"I was just talking to Kaya. And nothing. Just feminine products," she chuckled nervously.

"Feminine products, huh? You had to go out and buy more already when I just bought you some?" She started biting on her bottom lip and looked away from me. Something she did when she was nervous or lying. In this case, it looked like she was doing both.

"Yeah... Umm..." she trailed off, trying to get her lies together. I reached my hand out for the bag.

"Let me see the bag." She was hesitant, but she finally handed me the bag. She looked even more nervous than before as I grabbed the contents out of the bag. I couldn't believe what I had pulled out. I just stared at it, hoping my eyes were playing tricks on me. I was hoping this little box didn't say "Plan-B" on it. I looked up at her and she couldn't even look at me. She knew she was dead wrong for buying this shit. I had been telling her for the longest how I was ready to start a family and she goes and buys this bullshit ass pill?

"Damn, so you really don't want to have my baby, huh?" I asked, trying my hardest not to cuss her little ass out.

"It's complicated," she said barely above a whisper.

"What's so complicated about it? I nut in you, so you go out and buy a pill to kill the baby already? That's fucked up, Clay. That's real fucked up." I threw the box of pills on the counter and started to walk out of the kitchen. I was liable to put my hands on her ass so I had to get away from her.

"No, it's not like that!" she called after me. She ran after me and grabbed my hand.

"I'm just not ready to bring a baby into this world yet. We're not married and who knows if you're going to cheat on me again." I turned to look at her.

"So you're telling me that you're not ready to have a baby with me because you think I'm going to cheat? You got a ring on your finger, but you don't want to have a baby because we're not married? Aight, Clay. Take the pill then. Fuck my feelings, right?" I chuckled and made my way back up the stairs. I couldn't believe this shit. What's the point of still being with me if she didn't trust me at all? It's like she wanted me to cheat on her or something. Ever since I got caught over a year ago, I've been trying my hardest to prove to her that she's the only woman for me. I guess that still wasn't good enough for her, though. I knew one thing. If she took that pill, I don't know if I would be so quick to forgive her.

# Chapter Five: Kaya

I was tired as hell. I wasn't trying to do anything but lie in bed today. Well, lay in Mecca's bed. He was the other man that I was fucking and also getting money from. In my opinion, he was way better than Greg in the looks department and the sex department. That nigga had a monster between his legs and I couldn't get enough of it. If I did relationships, I would definitely consider making him mine, but I didn't have time for the drama that came along with the relationship.

Mecca was tall and dark chocolate, just like I liked them. He had a low cut and he always had a fresh line up. The tattoos that covered his body are what got my attention. He would always be in the strip club making it rain on my ass like there was no tomorrow. That was another thing that drew me to him. He was something serious.

My phone started ringing as I was laying on his chest. I didn't feel like moving at all, but it was probably important. I picked up my phone to see who was calling and it was Kevin.

"Yes, brother?" I answered.

"What you got planned for tonight?

"I gotta work at the club tonight, but other than that, I don't have anything planned."

"Good. We gotta hit a lick tonight." I perked up because now he was talking about making money.

"Word? Where at?"

"I'll give you the info later. I got shit to handle right now," he said.

"Aight, call me later." I ended the call and laid my head back down on Mecca's chest.

"So when are you gonna be mine?" Mecca asked. I rolled my eyes. It was always the same thing with him and Greg. They were always asking when I was going to stop playing games and be theirs. Umm, how about never?

"You know I don't do that relationship shit," I told Mecca.

"You keep saying that, but have you actually ever been in a relationship?"

"Nope. And I don't plan on it no time soon either. Why do you have a problem with what we're doing?" I asked.

"I didn't mean to catch feelings for you, Kaya. But I did. I know for a fact I'm not the only nigga you're fucking and that bothers me. Watching you shake your ass for all of those niggas at the club makes me want to kill all of them. I want you to myself." I got off of his chest and looked at him. Why did niggas always have to complicate shit? Why couldn't we just be fuck buddies and leave it at that?

"You shouldn't have caught feelings for me. I'm nothing great. I promise you," I let him know.

"You are to me. Don't tell me that after all this time that we've been fucking, you don't have some type of feelings for me."

"I mean, I care for you, but that's as far as it goes." He just nodded his head. I could tell that he wasn't feeling my answer at all. I told him that I wasn't looking for a relationship when we first started fucking around. I don't know why he was trippin' now.

My phone started ringing again and it was my best friend Clay calling. She had hung up on me earlier and I wasn't feeling that shit at all. I knew it was probably because of Rome, though, so I wasn't really mad at her.

"Oh, so now you decide to call me back?" I asked once I answered it.

"Shut up, bitch, he walked in on our conversation. Now he's all mad at me and shit and not talking to me. I need to get out of this house. You hungry? Let's go to Red Lobster."

"Shit, you know I'm down," I let her know.

"Okay. I'm about to call up Erica and tell her to meet us there too." I rolled my eyes at the mention of Erica's name. I wasn't a big fan of her. She was always throwing shade at me and shit. The only reason I haven't said anything to her was because she was friends with Clay. I wasn't going to let her keep sliding though. One of these days she was going to say some slick shit and I was going to hit her ass right in the mouth.

"Alright. I'll see you in about an hour." I hung up and got out of Mecca's bed.

"You're about to leave me already?" he asked.

"I've been with you all day. You'll see me again soon," I said, putting my clothes back on. He sat up in bed and smiled at me. He was so damn sexy.

"You better call me later. Stop using me for when you just want some dick." I laughed at him because that's exactly what I used him for.

"Okay, I'll call you," I lied. I kissed him on his cheek and grabbed the stack of money that was sitting on the dresser. I was out of his house before he could say anything else to me.

About an hour later, I was pulling into the parking lot of Red Lobster. I spotted Clay's all white BMW that Rome had gotten her for her birthday a couple of months ago. I made sure I parked right beside her car. I didn't expect her to still be in the car though. She looked over at me and I could tell she was stressing. She needed something to drink and fast.

"Hey, bitch, don't look so sad," I said once we were both out of our cars. She rolled her eyes and flipped her long hair over her shoulder. She had very light skin, compliments of her mixed ethnicity, with a beauty mark right above her top lip. Her hair stopped right in the middle of her back and when it was in its curly state, it stopped at her shoulders. Her breasts weren't the biggest, but she made up for that with that ass she was carrying around with her. That thing was huge!

"Come on, I'm hungry. I'm not waiting for Erica's slow ass," she said and we walked into the restaurant.

"So what happened? Why is he mad at you? Did he forget that you caught him in the club last night with Roxy's hoe ass on his lap?" I asked after the waitress took our order.

"He's mad because I'm not ready to have a baby with him. It's his fault that I don't trust him. He's the one that was fucking bitches in the house that we shared." I still didn't understand how niggas could do that. How could you bring a hoe to the house you shared with your fiancé? What sense did that make? None at all.

"I think you should've cut his ass. Niggas won't act right until you start to get violent with them," I let her know, taking a sip of my water.

"Last night, I bleached a lot of his clothes," she proudly stated.

"Oh shit. What did he do about that?"

"Girl, nothing. He acted like it didn't even bother him. I would expect him to be more upset over that and not this damn Plan-B pill. I just don't understand niggas," she shook her head.

"Damn, y'all bitches couldn't wait for me?" Erica's loud mouth ass said as she made her way to our table. I tried my hardest not to roll my eyes at her. I really wish Clay wouldn't have even invited her to come along, but I guess I was just going to have to suck it up and deal with her for now.

"You were taking too long and we were hungry," Clay told her. She sat down beside Clay and started looking through the menu.

"Anyways, before we were rudely interrupted," I said, cutting my eyes at Erica. "He doesn't care about the clothes because he knows that he can easily buy all of those back. Start putting your hands on him, girl. I promise you he'll start acting right."

"What? Clay, don't do that shit. What if he hits her back? Then what? She's going to be walking around with a black eye because she listened to your terrible advice," Erica said.

"That nigga ain't stupid enough to put his hands on me, first of all. And second, his ass will be in the hospital if he ever raises a hand at me," Clay let her know.

"Exactly. Unlike you, we actually know how to fight back when we need to defend ourselves. I'm shocked your ass ain't sporting around a black eye now," I chuckled.

"At least I got a man that loves me," she had the nerve to say. I couldn't help but laugh at her stupid ass.

"Girl, that's what you call love? Getting cheated on all of the time and getting your ass beat every night? Well, you can keep that shit," I chuckled again.

"You sure do have a lot to say for someone who can't even get a man." She rolled her eyes at me.

"Bitch, I don't need a man. All I need to do is make money. You're depending on your cheating ass nigga. How many STDs has that nigga given you? Oh, okay." Erica didn't say anything else because she knew her nigga wasn't shit. She thought she was better than everyone because she didn't work and her so-called boyfriend was taking care of her, but she was just a dumb ass if you asked me. She kept claiming that she had a man, but no one had ever seen his ass and she wouldn't tell us what his name was. The only reason we knew she had some type of nigga is because he was always beating her ass. That couldn't be me.

Erica wasn't an ugly chick at all. She had light brown skin, big brown eyes, and her hair was always done. She didn't have one of those bodies like a stripper at all. In fact, she was skinny as hell. She barely had breasts and her ass was as flat as a board. She could still get whoever she wanted because she had a pretty face. She preferred to settle for niggas she knew weren't shit. Clay tried talking to her about this plenty of times, but she wouldn't listen to her. I guess you really can't help someone who doesn't want to be helped.

"Kay, do you and Royal have something going on?" Clay asked me. Erica's face lit up at the mention of Royal's name.

"Who the fuck is Royal?" I asked.

"What? You don't know who Royal is?" Erica asked. She was acting like I had just committed a crime because I didn't know who Royal was.

"The nigga that was all up in your face last night at the club," Clay said, ignoring Erica.

"Oh, that nigga. We don't have shit going on. He was begging for my number and I wouldn't give it to him."

"Yeah right. Royal doesn't have to beg for shit. He can have whoever he wants. Why the hell would he be begging for your number out of all people?" Erica laughed. I wanted to hit her so bad right now. I just wanted to drag her ass out of the booth we were sitting in and beat her ass until she couldn't talk shit anymore.

"Well, I was just asking because he's been staring a hole through you since we sat down. It looks like he's on a date too. That is so disrespectful," Clay said, shaking her head. I slowly turned around and sure enough, it was the same nigga from the club last night staring right through my soul.

Damn, I don't remember him being this fine last night. He had the perfect shade of chocolate skin, his dreads were hanging past his shoulders and the ends of them were dyed dark green. Dark green? Out of all the colors, that's the one he chose? I had to admit though, the shit was sexy as hell, especially on him. I felt like he was the only nigga who could do some crazy shit like that and get away with it. I could see all of the tattoos that covered his arms, and then he smiled at me, showing a perfect set of white teeth. Oh goodness. I had to hurry and turn back around before he thought I was into him or something.

"Damn bitch, put your tongue back in your mouth," Clay said. I rolled my eyes at her.

"Girl, I'm not checking for that nigga," I said, waving her off.

"Well, it sure looks like he's checking for you. He's making his way over here right now." I felt myself getting hot. Why was he coming over here? He was here on a date with another female. I acted like I didn't even care that he was on his way to me. I kept drinking my water like everything was okay.

This nigga had the nerve to slide into the booth beside me like we knew each other personally and shit. His Versace cologne filled my nostrils, making me get horny instantly. I knew right then that I needed to stay away from this nigga. If he can make me wet just by being in my presence, imagine what that dick can do.

"What's good, Kaya?" he said, smiling at me. I rolled my eyes even though I wanted to smile back at him.

"Are you stalking me, Royalty?" I asked, getting his name wrong on purpose.

"It's Royal. And nah, we just happened to be at the same place at the same time. I think it was meant for you to give me your number."

"Nah, I'm good," I quickly said. I didn't want to give him my number. But then again, he had money. I could tell just by looking at him. All the ice that he was wearing around his neck was damn near blinding my ass. He laughed lightly.

"Well, take mine then," he said, reaching for my phone that was sitting on the table. I didn't even protest. I didn't have a password on my phone so he unlocked it and stored his number, then handed me my phone back.

"I expect to hear from you soon, Kaya," he said, standing up, then walking back to his table. This man had me so hot and bothered and he didn't even do anything but sit down next to me.

"I think he likes you," Clay said, smiling from ear to ear.

"Girl bye. He probably just wants one thing and that's to get inside my pants. I'm not thinking about that nigga, nor am I calling him," I let her know.

"He won't answer anyway. He never answers his phone," Erica chimed in. I could see it all over her face that she wasn't feeling how Royal had approached me. She was always hating, though. That's what she did best.

"How would you know? You got a man, don't you? What you doing calling Royal?" I asked with one of my eyebrows raised.

"I can have friends," she snapped and rolled her eyes. I knew exactly what that meant. Either she had fucked Royal or she wanted to. Either way, I didn't care. All I wanted out of that nigga was his money and that was it. She could have the nigga for all I cared.

*Later that night*

I sat in the passenger side of Kevin's car as we sat across the street from the house we were supposed to be robbing. I didn't even go to work tonight because I felt like this was more important. I liked the rush that breaking into people's homes gave me. It was like a high for me.

It was going on three o'clock in the morning and it was about that time to make our move. We wanted to make sure everyone in the house was sleeping before we went in. Kevin taught me how to pick a lock, so we didn't even have to worry about making too much noise with the door and waking them up. Even if they did wake up, it wouldn't be that big of a deal because I had no problems putting two bullets in someone's skull, then going on about my business.

"You ready?" Kevin asked me, making sure his gun was loaded.

"I'm always ready," I said, doing the same thing with my gun. We both pulled our ski mask down, then made our way towards the house. The houses in this neighborhood were big as hell. They were like mini mansions. One day, I was going to move into one of these. I couldn't wait for that day to come either.

Kevin and I went around to the back door because we felt like that would be easier. I picked the lock and we were in the house in no time. They didn't have an alarm system or anything. I felt like that was so stupid. You have all these nice things in your home, but don't feel the need to have an alarm system to protect all of your belongings? People like them needed to get robbed and people like me didn't have a problem doing it at all.

"Grab as much shit as you can. I'm not trying to be in here longer than fifteen minutes," Kevin whispered to me. I nodded my head and started picking up anything that looked like it was worth money. Whoever lived here clearly didn't care about their things that much. They had their jewelry laid out on the coffee table. Rings, necklaces, bracelets, all of that. Kevin grabbed the flat screen TV that was hanging on the wall while I grabbed the PS4 that they had, along with the two laptops that were also on the table. I grabbed the jewelry too and started making my way out the door.

"You see all the shit they had? Imagine what they'll have upstairs too. We should go back," I said.

"No. We're good for now. You want them mothafuckas to wake up? We came to steal, not kill," he said. I wasn't trying to hear that, though. I was money hungry. I wanted to get everything that I could so I could get even more money.

"Get in the car," Kevin demanded after he put the TV in the back of his Range Rover. I listened to him and got my ass in the car.

"There's a few other houses that we have to hit up, so get ya mind right," he told me. I couldn't stop the smile that spread across my face even if I wanted to. I guess the saying was right—money really does make me cum.

# Chapter Six: Erica

I really couldn't stand Kaya. She thought she was better than everyone, when in reality, she was nothing but a hoe. She was a borderline prostitute if you ask me. Who goes around fucking niggas for money? She is already a stripper, why was she prostituting on the side too? I didn't understand these bitches. Then she had the nerve to come for me earlier today about my relationship.

Just because Mecca puts his hands on me from time to time doesn't mean he doesn't love me. He always apologizes afterward anyway. I just need to learn how to stop making him so mad to the point he wants to hit me. It's always my fault because I'm always questioning him and I know he doesn't like that at all. Kaya needed to shut up and mind her business. I doubt that she'll ever find her a man that loves her as much as Mecca loves me.

I still couldn't believe Royal is checking for her ass. He didn't even acknowledge me when he came to our table. You would think that as much as I suck his dick, he would at least say hi to me or something. He ignored my ass like he didn't know me at all. I wasn't feeling that shit at all. As soon as we left Red Lobster, I planned on calling him to see what was up with him, but Mecca didn't come home, so I stayed up all night waiting for him.

He had the nerve to come home around eleven o'clock in the morning and ignore me. What was up with everyone acting like I didn't exist? That shit was really starting to piss me off.

"So you're just going to come in the house and act like I'm not sitting right here?" I asked with an attitude. He had just come out of the bathroom from taking a shower.

"Don't start with that shit. It's too damn early for you to be complaining," he said, walking over to the dresser so that he could put on some boxers.

"Complaining? Nigga, you didn't come home at all last night! You wouldn't even answer your phone!" I yelled, getting off of the bed. He ignored me as he put his boxers on. I hated when he acted like this. He acted like I was just some random chick and not his damn girlfriend.

"What bitch were you with last night? You might as well go stay with her ass since you don't know how to bring your ass home," I said.

"Shut the fuck up, Erica. This is why I don't come home! You always running your damn mouth. You never know when to stop flapping those damn gums of yours."

"Don't be mad when I start acting like you. Let's see how you like it when another nigga is feasting on my pussy while you're blowing up my phone and wondering where I am," I said, getting off of the bed so that I could go use the bathroom. Before I could make it to the bathroom, I felt myself being yanked back by my hair.

"You're gonna do what?" Mecca yelled as I hit the floor. I couldn't even respond to him because he punched me hard as hell in my face.

"You're always trying me, Erica! And you wonder why I'm always putting my hands on your stupid ass!" he yelled some more. At this point, I didn't even care what he was yelling about. I was too busy trying to get my nose to stop bleeding.

Mecca finished getting dressed and then left the house. I heard the front door slam and I couldn't do anything but cry. Mecca didn't used to be like this. At the beginning of our relationship, he was so loving, kind, and sweet. We used to do everything together. Once I started hanging out with Clay and Kaya, everything changed. I don't know what happened to him, but I want him to go back to the Mecca I fell in love with.

I got up enough strength to pull myself off of the floor and made my way into the bathroom. Mecca had only punched me once, but it looked like I had gotten into a fight with a group of girls. His punches were so damn powerful.

I had a busted lip, I had bruising under my right eye, and my nose was still bleeding. I tried my best to clean up my face because I had things planned for today. I didn't want to look a mess when I saw Royal today. I got excited just thinking about him. I didn't even care that Mecca had probably gone out to fuck another one of his bitches. Right now, he was the last thing on my mind.

I walked back into the bedroom to grab my phone off of the dresser. Most of the time Royal didn't answer my calls, but I was praying that he answered today. I needed to see him and ask him why he was checking for Kaya's hoe ass. I was going to tell him how she was basically a prostitute and maybe he wouldn't want to fuck with her anymore. He needs to be with me anyway. If he told me that he wanted me to be his, I would drop Mecca like a bad habit.

Dialing Royal's phone number, I anxiously waited for him to pick up. It rang more than once, so that was a good thing. Most of the time it rang once and then he sent it straight to voicemail. I don't know why he was always treating me like this.

"What, Erica?" he asked, sounding frustrated.

"Hey… Umm, I was wondering what you were doing?" I nervously said. I didn't expect him to answer this time. I didn't even rehearse what I was going to say to him.

"I'm handling business. Why?"

"Well, what are you doing later? I would really like to see you," I said, trying my best to sound sexy. He was quiet for a minute before he said something again.

"Aight, meet me at the Marriot in about an hour," he said, then ended the call. I was smiling like a Cheshire cat right now. I didn't even care that Mecca had just put his hands on me.

I walked into my closet so I could find something cute to wear. I couldn't just wear a regular outfit because I wasn't going to see a regular nigga. I had plenty of clothes to wear, but I didn't even wear half of them. Mecca was always sending me on shopping sprees. That was his way of apologizing for putting his hands on me and shit. I wasn't complaining at all because I loved shopping. Shit, if he had the money, I would gladly spend it.

I finally came across an all-white strapless dress that I had bought from Saks. The dress hugged my body, not really showing off any curves because I barely had them. I tried my hardest to gain weight, but it just never happened. I wanted to be thick like Kaya and Clay, but I guess it just wasn't meant to be.

After my shower, I curled my burgundy weave, beat my face for the gods, and then put on my dress. I was looking and feeling good. You couldn't even tell that Mecca had hit me and left bruises. I was thankful for that because I didn't want Royal to know that my boyfriend was beating my ass on the regular. He probably wouldn't care anyway, but I still didn't want him to know.

About thirty minutes later, I was pulling up to the Marriot hotel. I spotted Royal's all black Porsche as soon as I pulled into the parking lot. Every time I was with him, he drove a different car. He had so many that I had lost count. I loved how he was all about his money. I needed a nigga just like him.

I made sure I looked good before I got out of the car. I was looking like I was about to step onto the red carpet or something. I had even put on a pair of heels to make my outfit look even better. I was feeling confident as hell and I couldn't wait for Royal to see how I looked.

I didn't want to get in his car without warning, so I knocked on his tinted windows. They were so tinted that I couldn't even see inside of the car. Only Royal would do some shit like this. The window rolled down and a cloud of smoke hit me in the face.

"What the hell you waiting for? Get ya ass in the car," he demanded. He didn't have to tell me twice. I quickly opened the door and slid into the passenger seat. He was looking good as hell, like always. He wasn't even dressed up. All he was wearing was a plain white t-shirt and a pair of Nike joggers. It should be illegal for a man to look this damn good.

"Hey, Royal," I said happily.

"What's up? Why you got all that make up on lookin' stupid as hell?" he asked. I tried my hardest to act like what he said didn't hurt my feelings. I did all of this shit for him and he thinks it looks stupid? I thought I looked good.

"And why the hell you got on that outfit like your ass about to go straight to the club. Damn, all I'm doing is getting my dick sucked," he laughed.

"I wanted to look good for you," I said, still acting like his words didn't hurt.

"You wanted to look good for me, huh? Nah, I just think you wanted to hide them bruises that you probably got on your face. You got on so much makeup, your neck and face are two different colors," he said, shaking his head.

I was embarrassed as hell. Even he knew that Mecca was putting his hands on me. I knew I wasn't the best at doing makeup, but I didn't think it was that bad. I wanted to look at myself in the mirror, but I didn't want to let him know that his words had gotten to me.

"Your precious Kaya wears makeup all the time," I said, rolling my eyes at the thought of her.

"Your point?"

"You're over here talking shit about how you don't like my makeup, but she wears way more makeup than I do. You didn't think she looked stupid yesterday when you came to the table all up in her face. You were acting like you didn't even know who I was." I folded my arms across my chest because I really didn't like how he ignored me yesterday.

"She didn't look stupid at all. In fact, she looked like she was about to go to a photo shoot. That's a bad bitch. You should really take notes. Or get some tips or some shit."

"Nigga, I don't need to take any notes from that bitch!" I said louder than I meant to. I didn't need shit from Kaya. She wasn't shit but a hoe anyway. He chuckled at me and finished his blunt.

"Why would I need to take notes from a stripper?" I asked. He didn't even look bothered that I said she was a stripper.

"At least she's working for her money," he said.

61

"She's also fucking niggas for money too. That's probably what she's going to do to you if you start fucking with her." He didn't do anything but laugh.

"Damn, you sound like a hater to me."

"A hater? Nigga, please! Believe me, Kaya ain't nothing to hate on." Why did everyone think that bitch was so great? I was tired of that shit.

"Are you suckin' my dick or nah? I got other bitches that would love for me to call them up," he said. I wasn't about to pass this up. I loved sucking his dick. It was so big and I could barely fit the whole thing in my mouth.

I unzipped his pants and pulled out his semi-erect penis. I put the tip in my mouth, then went to work. He still seemed like he wanted Kaya and I didn't like that. I needed to find a way to make him not want to pursue her anymore. But what was it that I could do?

# Chapter Seven: Royal

It had been about a week and I still hadn't gotten that call from Kaya. I didn't like how she was acting like I was just some regular ass nigga or some shit. When I gave her my number, I expected her to call me that same day. These bitches would love for me to just give out my number. That's not something that I did very often. I ain't never been pressed over a bitch, but there was something about Kaya that wouldn't let me stop thinking about her.

I sat in the VIP section of the club that Kaya worked at. She was going to talk to me whether she wanted to or not. Once I got in her pants, I probably wouldn't even fuck with her like that, but right now, I needed to know how her pussy felt wrapped around my dick.

"Hey, Royal, would you like a dance?" this stripper named Roxy asked. She had been trying to fuck me for the longest, but the only thing I would let her do was suck my dick. She was a beast at that shit, so I called her up on the regular.

"Nah, but you can go find Kaya for me," I said. She didn't look too happy with my answer, but I didn't give a fuck. This shit wasn't about her. I was on a mission and if she wanted to be all up in my face, the least she could do was help a nigga out. I haven't seen Kaya since I've been here and I wasn't feeling that shit at all.

"What you want with her ass?" she asked with an eye roll.

"Don't fucking question me. Now go do what the fuck I said before I stop calling your ass when I need my dick sucked." That was all she needed to hear. She hurried out of my section and went to find Kaya. I inhaled the smoke from the blunt I was smoking and sat back and waited.

"Nigga, I would appreciate if you wouldn't ask for me by name in here. My name is Honey. Now, what do you want?" Kaya asked once she was in my section. She was looking good enough to eat. In fact, that's exactly what I wanted to do right now. I wasn't even into eating bitches' pussies. Kaya looked like she tasted sweet as hell and I couldn't wait to try it out either.

"Your name is whatever the fuck I call you. Now give me a dance," I demanded. She rolled her eyes and folded her arms across her chest.

"Didn't your mom teach you any manners? Don't be demanding me to do shit," she snapped. I could tell that I was going to have some fun with her. I wasn't even worried about her attitude problem. That's nothing that I can't fix.

"Give me a dance, please," I said, pulling a stack out of my pocket. She smirked before coming closer to me and putting her ass in my lap. She smelled good as hell. Maybe like strawberries or some shit. Watching her twerk her ass had my dick hard as hell. I needed to get inside of her guts and fast. She was the best dancer in this club. I would come here every night just to get a dance from her. That's some real shit.

I was a little mad when the song was over and she stopped dancing. She bent down to grab her money that I had thrown at her, but I pulled her body closer to mine. Once her face was a few inches from mine, I stuck my tongue down her throat. She didn't stop me like I thought she would, so I kept kissing her. Her breath smelled like mints. Like she had just eaten one or she had just finished chewing a piece of minty gum. My dick was begging to be released, but I had to contain myself.

I pulled away and smiled at her. She looked like she was in a daze from what I had just done. Shit, I shocked myself by doing it too. I didn't kiss bitches. I didn't know whose dick they had been sucking and shit like that. I felt like that shit wasn't sanitary at all.

"I gave you my number for a reason, but you must've forgotten or some shit. So here's what I'm gonna do. I'm going to hand you my phone and you're going to put your number in that bitch. If I call you and you don't pick up, we're going to have a serious issue. Do you understand me?" I asked. She nodded her head and I took out my phone and handed it to her. She quickly stored her number in it and handed the phone back to me. Once she did that, she picked up the rest of her money and hurried out of my section.

I had finally broken down that wall that she had built up for no reason. I liked that she wasn't a thirsty bitch though. I couldn't stand those kinds of bitches. If a nigga isn't showing any type of interest in you, why are you still trying? I didn't understand these bitches man. They did the absolute most.

The next morning, I woke up and got dressed. I was going to see what was up with these traps. I had to make sure they were running smoothly and all of my money was coming in how it was supposed to be. I was making plenty of money. I could get out of the game right now if I wanted and I would be set for the rest of my life. I wanted to open up a couple of businesses first. After I did that, I wouldn't be fucking with this shit like that no more. I didn't like risking my freedom anymore. I was getting too old for that shit.

Pulling up to the trap house, I spotted someone I didn't expect to see. My ex-girlfriend, Paisley. I was confused as to why she was on this side of town and why she was at the trap house. Paisley wasn't the type to hang out in the hood at all. She hated when we would even ride through the hood. She always claimed that she was afraid that she was going to get shot at and how she was too young to die. She was scary as fuck and that shit got on my nerves.

I met Paisley when I was at the gas station one day. I was standing in line behind her and she was trying to put two dollars in her gas tank. I didn't know her or anything, but it sounded to me like she was struggling. I decided to be a gentleman and put twenty dollars in her gas tank. I only did it because she looked good as hell. She had dark skin, medium length hair, and an average body. She didn't seem stuck up at all and I could fuck with that.

After I paid for her gas, we exchanged numbers and one thing led to another and we ended up dating. At first, everything was all good. She would cook for me, clean the house, and gave me pussy whenever I wanted it. Let's not forget to mention that she was a beast at giving head. She gave the best head ever, and I ended up cutting off some of my hoes for her.

Everything was good until one day she went through my phone and saw that I was still fucking other bitches. I'm a man, so what did she expect? She went crazy as hell. She tried to destroy all of my clothes, but I caught her in the act and made her ass get the hell out of my house. I didn't understand what the big deal was. Yeah, I was fucking other females, but she was the one that I came home to every night. That wasn't enough for her though.

After we broke up, she wanted to get back together. I wasn't feeling that shit though. I felt she was acting too crazy for me so I was good single. I would still fuck her from time to time, but I had to stop doing that too because she would start thinking that we were together again. She would start popping up on my ass every time I was with another female. That crazy bitch was following me and I didn't like that shit.

I had to threaten to end her life in order for her to stop following me. She cried and begged for me back, but she was too damn crazy for me. She even went as far as telling me that she was going to kill herself if I didn't take her back, and I told her to do what she had to do. I know it sounds fucked up, but she wasn't my problem anymore.

I got out of my car and made my way into the trap house. My workers were always on point doing what they were supposed to be doing, so I wasn't worried about that. I popped up all of the time and they knew if they weren't working, I wouldn't hesitate to murk a nigga. It's been done before.

"What's up, Boss Man?" this young nigga named Jay asked. He looked nervous as shit. His eyes kept shifting from the back room back to me. I knew something was up because he wouldn't be acting like this. I ignored his ass and went straight into the back room, gun drawn and all. I didn't know what to expect when I got back there, so I just made sure I was prepared.

I tried opening the door, but the bitch was locked. *What the fuck?* These niggas were really trying me today. I chuckled to myself before kicking the door down. What I saw was a surprise of a lifetime. Paisley was naked as the day she was born and on her knees, giving this nigga named Sean head.

"Oh shit, Royal!" he said, fumbling to pull his pants up. Paisley didn't even look like herself. Her hair was a mess, she was skinny as hell, and she looked like she was homeless. She didn't even look like the girl I once had deep feelings for. I've seen this plenty of times though. I knew that she was on drugs. That's exactly how my aunt started looking before she contracted AIDS from a needle and died.

"The fuck is going on in here?!" I yelled.

"Royal, man… It's not what you think," he said, fumbling over his words. Paisley was trying to put her clothes back on as quickly as possible. She wouldn't even look at me.

"Then what the fuck is it? You in here fucking when you need to be working!" I didn't know if I was more upset with the fact that he was in here basically about to fuck my ex, or if it was the fact that she was in here looking like she was about to die at any moment.

"She didn't have the money to pay for the dope she wanted and she told me that she would work it off, so I figured why not have some fun with this and—"

*POW! POW! POW!*

I didn't even want to hear him finish this story. I shot him three times in the head to shut his ass up. I was that pissed off. Paisley saw what I had done and she started screaming at the top of her lungs. I grabbed her by the collar of her shirt and brought her face close to mine.

"Shut the fuck up before I do the same to you," I said through gritted teeth. She immediately stopped screaming. She looked like she was scared as hell, but I honestly didn't care. Paisley had things going for her in life. I was mad as hell that she had turned to drugs. She was better than that.

"Let's go," I demanded, walking out of the room. Jay was still looking nervous as hell and I didn't blame him. He probably thought I was going to kill his ass next, but I wasn't. I had bigger things on my agenda and that was tending to Paisley.

"It's a situation upstairs. Handle that," I said, walking out of the house with Paisley right behind me. I knew Jay would probably call the cleanup crew to get rid of Sean's body.

"Where are you taking me? I want to go home," Paisley said once we were both in my car. I didn't give a fuck what she wanted to do right now. What she needed to do was shut the fuck up before I put my hands on her. That's really how I was feeling right about now.

"Shut the fuck up, Paisley. Everything isn't about you. You think I wanted to walk in on my ex giving head because she couldn't pay for drugs? Nah, I didn't, but you don't hear me bitching about shit," I snapped. She looked like I had hurt her feelings, and I hoped I did. She knew what she was doing wasn't cool at all.

"If I would've known that you were going to show up, I would've just waited." She had the nerve to have an attitude with me. I clenched my teeth together and turned up the music. She was pissing me off more and more. I needed her to stop talking.

About twenty minutes later, I pulled up to my apartment that I only used for fucking bitches because I didn't want them to know where I really lived. Paisley looked like she didn't want to get out of the car, but she quickly got out when she saw me walking up to the building.

"Why are we here? I need to go back to my mom's," she said, walking behind me. I didn't care about all of that, though. I didn't want her to go back to her mom's crib because I already knew that her mom was the reason Paisley was on drugs now. Her mom, Betty, was a known crack head. Paisley usually stayed away from her, but I didn't know what had been going on for these past two years.

"You ain't going back to your mom's crib, so you can get that shit out of your head right now," I said as I unlocked the door. I heard her smack her lips, but I still didn't give a fuck about the little attitude that she had. She was just mad because she wouldn't be able to get drugs like she wanted.

"Make yourself at home. You'll be living here once you come back from rehab," I let her know.

"WHAT? I'm not going to rehab! I don't even need it! I'm not a drug addict, Royal! Stop acting like I am!" she yelled.

"I don't know who the fuck you think you yelling at, but you need to cut that shit out. I guess those drugs must've made you forget who the fuck I am."

"I'm sorry, Royal. I'm not going to rehab." She folded her arms across her non-existent breast like that was going to do something. She really thought that I was going to change

71

my mind about this, but I wasn't. I didn't want to see her throw her life away like my auntie did and I also didn't want her to die, so she was going to rehab. I guess a small part of me still cared about her ass.

"Yes, you are. End of discussion," I said, sitting down on the couch and pulling out my phone. I had planned to call Kaya right after I left the trap house, but Paisley fucked that up for me. That lap dance she gave me last night had been on my mind since I woke up this morning. I decided to call her now since I wasn't doing anything.

"Hello?" she answered on the first ring.

"Damn girl, you must've been waiting for me to call. You didn't even let the bitch ring all the way," I laughed.

"Boy bye. I had my phone in my hand, so of course I'm going to answer it as soon as it starts ringing. You ain't nobody special. Don't flatter yourself." It was something about the way she talked to me that got my dick hard. Most of these bitches were too afraid to talk to me any kind of way. I didn't blame them, though. They knew not to try me.

"You were waiting for me to call you. You don't have to lie. But anyway, what you doing tonight?"

"I work at night," she stated like I was supposed to know that she worked every night.

"Well, take tonight off."

"Taking nights off doesn't bring in money. You gonna pay me for missing work?" She was all about her money and I was too. She and I would be the perfect team.

"Yep. I'll even double it," I said it before I could catch myself. I don't give money to these bitches. The fuck was wrong with me?

"Shit, then I'm down for whatever. Where you trying to chill at?"

"We can just chill at your crib, ma." She was quiet for a minute like she didn't want me to come to her spot or something.

"Okay. I'll text you the address. Just let me know when you're on the way," she finally said.

"Aight, cool." I didn't know why, but I was feeling all bubbly inside. No girl had ever had that effect on me.

"Who the fuck is that bitch you were just talking to? She must be fucking you real good if she's got you over there smiling like that," Paisley said. I had forgotten that she was even in the same room with me.

"Don't worry about me. You need to be worried about getting your life together and getting off them damn drugs. That shit ain't a good look on you," I said, standing up so that I could leave.

"Where are you going? You're just going to leave me here by myself so you can go fuck another bitch?" she asked. Here we go with this crazy shit. She was acting like I was her nigga already.

"I'm going to mind my fucking business. You should try it. There's food in here. You know how to cook so that shouldn't be a problem for you. Don't leave this fucking house, Paisley. I'm dead ass," I said, looking at her in her eyes so that she would know I was serious.

"Don't be gone all night. You know I don't like being in the dark by myself," she said. I chuckled and left out of the apartment. I had to go home and get fresh. I was planning on being all up in Kaya's guts tonight. I couldn't wait to brag about what her pussy game is like because I know it's something serious.

# Chapter Eight: Kaya

I was smiling so hard after that phone call with Royal. I had been thinking about him since last night. I didn't expect him to kiss me like that. I also didn't expect for the kiss to have that effect on me either. That had never happened to me before. I kiss niggas all the time and that's exactly what it is. Just a kiss. It wasn't that with Royal, though. That nigga had me feeling like we were the only people in the room. I swear I heard birds chirping too.

After I gave him that dance, I couldn't do anything else. My head was all fucked up. The manager of the club thought I was sick, but I wasn't. My panties were wet and I was in a daze. I just went home after that. I couldn't focus on anything but Royal. He was consuming all of my thoughts, and still is.

I admit I had been waiting for him to call me all day. I was starting to think that he wasn't going to call me and my feelings were a little hurt. Most of the time, I didn't care about these niggas. They were usually the ones that would be sitting at home waiting for my phone call. It was never the other way around. Royal was something serious and I don't know if I was going to be able to handle a man like him. He was different from these other niggas that I fucked with. He was the true definition of a boss.

"Kevin, I need you to leave. I got company coming over," I said, walking into Kevin's room. He was laid out on his bed, watching TV.

"How you gonna put me out of my house just because you're trying to have some nigga over," he said, not even looking at me. I rolled my eyes at him.

"He's more than just some nigga. Can you please leave?"

"More than just some nigga? Let me find out little Kaya got feelings," he laughed. I didn't find shit funny though. I just needed him to leave.

"Shut the hell up. Are you leaving or not?"

"Nah. I'll stay in my room."

"Fine. If you want to hear me moaning all night… Don't say I didn't warn you."

"Man, hell nah. I'm leaving. I'll find some shit to do," he said, getting off of his bed. I smiled and walked out of his room and back to mine. I didn't know what time he planned on coming over, but I needed to find something to wear. Right after I called Clay and told her the good news.

"Hello?" she answered the phone sounding stressed as hell.

"Girl, guess what?" I damn near yelled.

"What?"

"Royal is coming over tonight!"

"Damn bitch, you don't have to yell. And I knew you wanted that nigga. I don't know why the hell you were frontin' so damn hard."

"Be quiet. I don't want him. I just want his money," I said, trying to convince myself that I didn't want anything from Royal but his money and dick.

"Keep lying to yourself, girl. Even I can see that isn't all you want from him. You want his last name and to carry all of his kids." I couldn't help but laugh at her ass.

"Girl bye. Nothing is coming out of this pussy," I said, meaning every word.

"If you say so. Let me know how your night goes. I want all of the details too."

"You know I gotchu," I said. We said our goodbyes and I ended the call. I felt like I was too anxious for Royal to come over, so I decided to roll a blunt to calm myself down and take a thirty-minute nap. After that, I would go to the mall and find me something to wear so I could look better than I usually did.

I woke up to my phone ringing. It was getting dark outside and I realized that my thirty-minute nap turned into a five-hour nap. Shit. I looked at my phone and saw that it was Royal calling, so I quickly answered it.

"Hello?" I said groggily into the phone.

"Damn, I know your ass ain't over there sleep. It's early as hell, girl," he said. This nigga even sounded delicious on the phone.

"I took a nap," I let him know.

"Well, wake that ass up. And send me that address too. I'll be over in about an hour."

"Okay," I said and hung up. I quickly threw the covers off of me and went to get in the shower. I couldn't believe that I had slept for so long. I didn't even know that I was that tired. I was mad at myself because I really wanted to go to the mall and find me something cute to wear. I guess I was just going to have to find me something to wear in my closet. I had plenty of clothes anyway.

After my shower, I straightened my weave and made sure it was bone straight before going to the closet to find something cute to wear. As I was looking through my clothes, I realized I was doing too much. I had never tried this hard to impress a nigga, and I wasn't about to start now. This nigga already had me acting out of character and we hadn't even had sex yet.

I decided to just wear a tank top and some small shorts that were comfortable as hell. I didn't feel like putting on any makeup, so I didn't. Royal had never seen me without makeup, so I didn't know how he was going to react when he saw me today. I put lotion on my legs and arms, then I went to sit on the couch. Kevin wasn't here and I was glad that he left. I didn't need him around being nosey and shit. This is why I never brought any niggas over to the house. I would much rather go to their house, get some dick, then come back home. It was easier that way.

About thirty minutes later, there was a knock at the door. My heart rate sped up and my palms started sweating. Why the hell did this nigga have me so nervous? This wasn't normal for me at all.

It didn't help at all that Royal was standing there looking like a tall glass of chocolate milk. He was looking at me like he wanted to bend me over, and he probably did. My ass was hanging out of the bottom of my shorts and I wasn't wearing a bra. I did that on purpose.

"You gonna let a nigga in or what?" he asked with a sexy ass smirk on his face. I stepped to the side to let him in, then closed the door behind him. He even smelled good as hell, but that was expected. He smelled good the last two times I was in his presence. He was already making me wet and he hadn't laid a finger on me.

"This is a nice place you got here. You live here by yourself?" he asked, sitting down on the couch.

"No, I live with my brother. He pays for everything." I sat down beside him.

"So, you just make that money down at the club and don't even help out with the bills?" Royal laughed.

"Pretty much. It's not that I don't want to help out; he won't let me. Believe me, I tried." I shrugged my shoulders. I didn't complain about not being able to pay bills. That was more money in my pockets.

"You not gonna offer a nigga anything to drink? You're a rude ass host," he joked.

"Damn, I forgot how thirsty your ass is. Let me go see what we got in there." I got off the couch and I could feel his eyes on my ass as I made my way into the kitchen. I didn't know what it was that he wanted to drink, so I just got the bottle of Cîroc and two glasses for us.

"Do you drink this?" I asked, sitting down.

"Not really, but I will if it's all you got." It wasn't all that we had. Kevin kept us stocked with liquor, but I wasn't going to tell Royal that. I didn't feel like getting back up. I opened the bottle and poured me some. I didn't want to get too drunk, I just wanted a little buzz. There's no telling what I might end up saying to this man if I was drunk. I had no type of filter.

"So tell me about yourself, Kaya," he said, pouring him something to drink.

"There's not much to know. I'm twenty, and I make money. That's literally my life," I chuckled.

"Nah, that can't be it. Tell me about your childhood and shit. How it was growing up." I didn't want to tell him that my mom wasn't shit. I didn't want to tell him that I had no high school education, and I damn sure didn't want to tell him that in order for me to start getting money I had to start robbing niggas and stripping. I didn't know him like that. He probably really didn't care anyway. He was just trying to make conversation.

"That's not something I like sharing with people," I said. He nodded his head and left it alone. I was glad too.

"What about you? Tell me about yourself." I drunk my drink.

"I'm twenty-five and I make money," he said, copying me. I laughed at him.

"Whatever, nigga. What made you want to dye the ends of your dreads green?"

"I lost a bet and I had to dye it some weird color that you don't really see, so I went with green. I was only going to keep it for like a week, but I started liking it and now I just keep it how it is. I might dye them back black, but I don't know yet. I'm not trying to impress these bitches." I raised my eyebrow at him.

"Oh, you're not?"

"Nope. Never have and never will."

He and I talked for hours. We even drank the whole bottle of Cîroc. Something that I really didn't mean to do at all. I didn't even feel drunk until my ass stood up and fell down on his lap. I was a little embarrassed, but all I could do was laugh at myself.

"I'm going to the bathroom," I said, standing back up.

"I'm coming with you." He stood up and followed me upstairs to my room. There was a bathroom downstairs, but I liked using mine. I rarely ever went into that bathroom.

Royal was sitting on my bed when I came out of the bathroom. Was it possible that he was looking better than before? I had to look away from him to control the nasty thoughts that were going on in my head.

"Come here," he said, motioning me towards him. I did exactly what he asked, but I didn't expect him to pull me down on the bed with him.

"You play too—" I started to say, but before I could, he stuck his tongue down my throat the same way he did the night before at the club. Oh goodness. My heart rate sped up again and I felt myself getting moist between my legs. I didn't want the kiss to end, just like last night. I never experienced this feeling before and I was loving it. I was loving it a little too much. I moaned into his mouth, and he pulled away and looked at me.

No words were spoken between the two of us as he started removing my clothes. I wasn't even going to stop him because I wanted this just as bad as he did. Once my clothes were removed, he started doing the same for him. His body was perfect. The tattoos that covered his torso made him even more attractive. This man was too damn fine.

He spread my legs apart and stuck two fingers inside of me. I guess he was satisfied with what he felt because he removed his fingers and replaced them with his thick dick. I had never been with a man that was this long and this thick. He was having trouble getting it in.

I gasped once he finally entered me. This shit was so painful. I felt like I was a virgin again.

"Wait, Royal! It hurts!" I yelled, trying to push him off of me. He was too heavy though and he wasn't going anyway.

"Chill girl, I got you," he said, slowly pumping in and out of me. He had his eyes closed and I could tell that he was really enjoying this. I could've came just from looking at his sex faces.

Royal started going faster and it started feeling good. This was another feeling that I had never experienced before. What was this man doing to my ass?

"Shit," Royal whispered. I could tell that he was trying his hardest not to moan and it was cute. I, on the other hand, was screaming at the top of my lungs.

"Yess, Royal! Don't stop! I'm about to cum!" He wrapped his hand around my throat and I came all over his dick. I had never been fucked like this. The niggas I was fucking with didn't have shit on Royal. This was a whole new level of euphoria. I could feel him in my stomach, rearranging my insides. I knew I probably wouldn't be able to walk tomorrow.

"Fuckkk!" Royal yelled. My eyes started rolling into the back of my head as I felt myself about to cum again. Damn, already? This man was dangerous.

"Shittt!" I yelled as I came again. His strokes became harder and harder until he screamed out. I didn't expect him to yell that loud, but he did. He fell over on top of me. I couldn't even say anything to him. I was having a hard time keeping my eyes open. Before I knew it, I was out like a light.

The next morning, I woke up in bed beside Royal. This never happened before. No one had spent the night. I don't even spend the night with niggas. He must've really put it down last night for me to just fall asleep like that. I sat up in bed and looked over at him. Even in his sleep, he still looks good as hell. Ugh!

I got out of bed and went to go relieve my bladder. Once I came out of the bathroom, Royal was awake and putting his clothes on.

"You're leaving so soon?" I asked.

"Yeah, I wasn't supposed to spend the night. I got business to handle. I'll hit you up later, though," he said, giving me a quick peck on the lips, then leaving my room. I didn't know why, but I was sad that he had left. I sat down on the bed and pouted.

"Bitch, what the hell you in here all sad about?" Clay said, coming into my room.

"When the hell did you get here?" I asked.

"Kevin let me in like an hour ago. I had to get out of the house before I go crazy. Now tell me all about your night with Royal." She smiled, coming to sit on the bed beside of me.

I told her all about my night with Royal. I made sure I didn't leave out any of the details.

"Wait, so you had sex with that nigga and you didn't even ask him for money?" she asked, sounding shocked as hell.

"Money was the last thing that was on my mind while he was inside of me." I was even shocked at myself. Most of the time, I wouldn't even get undressed until I saw the money first. Everything was different with Royal, though. I didn't know what it was, I just knew that he was dangerous. I had to make sure that I kept a straight head on when I was around him. If not, I might fuck around and catch feelings, and I didn't have time for that at all.

# Chapter Nine: Clay

I loved Rome with all of my heart. He was the best thing that's ever happened to me, but he was still ignoring me and it was starting to get old. I understood that he was mad about me buying that Plan-B pill, but I didn't even take it. I guess that wasn't enough for him, though. He wanted me to kiss his ass and beg him to talk to me and I didn't want to do that.

I guess I was going to have to be the bigger person in this whole situation and go talk to him. I hated being ignored, especially when I didn't do anything wrong. I even told him that I didn't take the pills and threw the whole box away in front of him, but that still wasn't enough for him. He still wouldn't talk to me. He was acting really childish and I was starting to get tired of it.

After I had left Kaya's house, I decided to go to the tattoo shop so that Rome and I could talk. I was going to let him know that I was tired of this bullshit. We are two adults; why the hell couldn't we talk out our problems? He was making things so much worse.

Pulling up to the shop, I took a deep breath before I got out of the car. I really hope that Rome would talk to me and not ignore me like I wasn't standing there. That would really hurt my feelings and I was tired of that. I wish he didn't have such a huge effect on my feelings, but he did.

As I walked through the doors of his shop, everyone that was waiting turned to look at me. They were acting like I had some type of disease or something. I wasn't feeling this at all.

"Nice to see you, Clay," his receptionist Brandi said. I rolled my eyes at her. She had a crush on Rome and he kept acting like he didn't know it. I could tell by the way she looked at him. I wouldn't hesitate to beat anyone's ass, so she better leave my nigga the fuck alone.

"Where's Rome?" I asked, placing my hand on the desk so that she could see my huge engagement ring. Once she looked at my hand, I could tell that she was bothered, but she still tried to keep it professional.

"He's in his office," she said. Once I started walking towards the back, I heard her mumble something under her breath, but I wasn't in the mood to entertain her right now. I had more important things to take care of and it didn't involve her.

As I walked into Rome's office, I saw him sitting on his desk and some bitch was standing behind him, giving him a back rub. This nigga here! He wonders why I'm always acting crazy and popping up on him and shit, and this is the reason why! If I even thought about letting another nigga put his hands on me, he would lose his damn mind. He would kill whoever the nigga was and probably try to kill me too.

"Hi, can we help you?" the girl had the nerve to ask. Rome had his eyes closed because I guess he was really enjoying the massage this bitch was giving him. Looking the girl in the face, I knew exactly who she was. She was the same bitch that he cheated on me with in our house. The nerve of this nigga. She had a smirk on her face like she knew who I was. I think she did though. I beat her ass one time, and I guess I was going to have to do it again.

I didn't say anything as I approached her. The fact that she was still massaging my man and his eyes were still closed because he was enjoying it that much had me seeing red. It must still be something going on between the two of them because why the hell did he feel the need to still talk to a bitch that almost cost him his relationship? It's obvious that I wasn't that important to him and that shit hurt.

Before the bitch could even react, I punched her ass right in the mouth and she went crashing down to the floor. I got on top of her and started punching her repeatedly until I blacked out. The last thing I remember was Rome pulling me off of her and trying to calm me down. There was no calming me down. He really had me fucked up.

Looking at the girl, I had really fucked her up. She wasn't an ugly girl at all, but now you couldn't even tell. Both of her eyes were swollen shut, she had a big ass knot in the middle of her forehead, she had scratches all over her cheeks, and she was bloody as hell. She was out cold. I really did a number on her, but she deserved it. She knew Rome was in a relationship. She knew when she thought it was okay to fuck him in my house. I guess bitches never learn though.

"Chill, Clay. You're going to kill that girl," he said into my ear. For some reason, that pissed me off even more. I snatched away from him and looked at his stupid ass.

"So you really think it's okay for you to be back here getting massages from the same bitch you fucked in my house?!" I yelled. I could tell by the look on his face that he didn't expect me to remember who she was, but what woman would forget something like that?

"It's not even like that," he tried to plead his case. "Take your ass home and we can talk once I get there." He was looking at his little bitch the whole time he said that. It was obvious that there was still something going on between the two of them and that infuriated me even more. Why was he so worried about her? Why didn't he care about his so-called fiancé that was standing right in front of him, blowing steam out of her ears?

That's when a thought popped into my head. Kaya said niggas will never learn until you put your hands on their stupid ass. Without even thinking, I drew my hand back and slapped the shit out of him. From the look on his face, I could tell that he was shocked at what I had just done. I'd never put my hands on him before. To be honest, that shit felt good as hell. I decided to do it again, but this time, with a closed fist. I punched him until I saw that he was bleeding. He was trying to block the punches coming at him, but he couldn't. I was like a raging bull right now. Nothing could stop me.

"Since she's so important to you, be with her. Maybe she'll marry your stupid ass and put up with the bullshit because I'm done," I let him know. He looked at me like he didn't believe me because I had told him that I was done before, and what did I always do? Come right back to his ass.

"She's not important to me. She's just a friend." I slapped him again because he really thought that I was stupid. Anyone with eyes could tell it was deeper than that. Maybe not for him, but it was for her. I could see it in her eyes. Before I knew it, I was crying like a big ass baby.

"Clay…" Rome said, trying to hug me while he was still holding his bleeding nose.

"Get the fuck off of me!" I started swinging at him again, and the next thing I knew, I was being thrown to the ground and handcuffs were being slapped on my wrist. Wow. Someone had really called the police and now they're taking my ass to jail.

Rome followed us the whole way out of his shop. All eyes were on us as they hauled me off like I was a criminal. I locked eyes with Brandi and from the look on her face, I knew she was the one who had called the police. After I got out of jail, I was coming back for her ass. She didn't even know that she had just started a war between the two of us.

"I'll get you out as soon as I can, bae," Rome said as they were putting me in the back of the squad car.

"Don't bother. Go make sure I didn't kill your little girlfriend," I spat. The rude ass police officer slammed the door so that we couldn't talk anymore. Rome's face was messed up too, but not as bad as ole girl's was. He had a busted lip and a black eye. His nose was still bleeding too. I was happy that I had fucked his beautiful face up like that. I didn't know that I even had that in me.

I was done playing with Rome's ass. Let's see how he likes it when I started acting like him. Let's see how he acts when he finds me sitting on a nigga's lap or if another nigga gives me a massage and I say, "Oh, he's just a friend". I was starting to think this relationship wasn't worth it anymore. Why would he keep doing shit like this if he loved me? I wasn't any better. I would take him right back after he did some shit. That's why he kept thinking it was okay to do what he does. There's some things you just don't do in a relationship out of respect for your partner. Obviously, his ass didn't know that though.

I felt like I was in that nasty ass jail forever. I was thankful when they gave me my one phone call. I called Kaya's ass right up. She told me that she was with Royal, but she was about to be on her way. She wanted to know what happened, but I didn't feel like explaining that shit over the phone. I was just ready to get the hell out of here. I wasn't going back to that house that I shared with Rome. We needed some time apart. I wasn't even going to talk to him. The fact that he thought it was okay to get touched on by a female that he cheated on me with was crazy to me. I shook my head just thinking about it.

"Williams, you made bail," the fat lady officer said. I wanted to jump for joy. I was ready to run out of this terrible place. I had never been so happy to see Kaya before in my life. I ran right to her and gave her a hug. I was shocked to see that Royal had come with her. She usually just left niggas where they were if I called with an emergency.

"Are you okay? No one tried to rape you, right?" she asked as we walked out to Royal's car.

"I'm good. I'm just over the bullshit," I replied honestly.

"So what the hell happened? Who called the police on you?"

"The stupid receptionist that works at Rome's tattoo shop. I went there to talk to Rome because he has been ignoring me and shit, and when I go into his office, he has some bitch giving him a fucking massage. Oh, and she's not just some bitch. She's actually the bitch that he cheated on me with in our house last year," I let her know, shaking my head. I still couldn't believe that this shit had even happened.

"What?! You beat both of their asses, right?" she asked in disbelief.

"Yep. That's how I ended up in jail. I'm so done with Rome. He's not even worth it anymore." Kaya looked at me like she didn't believe me, but I was so serious. There were plenty of fish in the sea. I wasn't ugly at all either, so I knew that I would be able to find someone that's even better than Rome. The only problem was I didn't want to do that. I wanted to get married to that man and have his babies. I guess things don't always work out the way you want them to.

Kaya dropped me off at my house and I was glad that Rome's car wasn't in the driveway. That would give me plenty of time to get my things packed and go to my mom's house. My mom didn't like Rome at all. She never liked him. Even when we first got together back when I was in high school. She claimed she didn't like him because he was a drug dealer. He stopped selling drugs and became a tattoo artist. She still didn't like that. He even opened up his own tattoo shop. She doesn't like that either. She claims that I needed to be with someone who's a lawyer or a doctor. That's not what I wanted, though. I wanted to be with Rome.

It took me about thirty minutes to pack the things that I would need. This was a normal thing for me. Rome and I would get into it and I would pack my things and go to my mom's house. It was starting to get tiring, though. I was thinking about just getting my own apartment or something because I didn't want to hear my mom's mouth every time I came over there. Good or bad terms, she always had something negative to say about Rome.

When I pulled up to my mom's house, all of the lights were off and I was happy about that. Maybe she was sleep and I wouldn't have to hear her mouth tonight. All I wanted to do was take a shower and watch movies for the rest of the night.

"I was wondering how long it was going to take you to show up here again. What's that nigga done this time? Cheat on you again?" my mom said as soon as I entered the house. She was sitting on the couch watching TV. I was hoping like hell she would've been asleep. This is what she greets me with. Not a simple "hi" or "how are you".

"I just needed some space," I said, walking past her and into my old room. Of course, she had to follow me.

"You just needed some space, huh? Why? What has he done this time?"

"It's not important," I said, hoping she would just leave the whole thing alone. I was not about to let her know that I spent half of my day in jail because of him. I'm not letting her know anything. All she was going to do is tell me how he wasn't good enough for me and bullshit like that.

"It's something if it got you at my house. I know you, Clay. So what bitch was he fucking with this week?" I rolled my eyes because she really wasn't giving up. I was over her right now.

"There isn't another woman, mom. Now could you please leave so that I can go to sleep?" She chuckled, then walked out of the room. I knew she would bring it right back up in the morning. She didn't know how to let stuff go for some reason. I was starting to wish that I would've never told her about Rome cheating on me because she keeps bringing the shit up. I was just tired of everything right now. I really needed a vacation by myself. Then maybe when I came back, I could deal with the bullshit. That sounded like a great plan.

# Chapter Ten: Rome

It seemed like I couldn't do anything right when it came to Clay. I didn't expect her to just pop up at the shop like that. Nikki had come to the shop to see how I was doing. I know I should've sent her on her way when she showed up, but she was a really cool person to hang around. That's where I fucked up the first time. I used to chill with Nikki on some friend type shit, but then one day she had come to my crib to give me my phone that I had left at her place. She was looking good as hell; I couldn't deny that. She had the body of a goddess and she was wearing a tight ass dress that didn't help me at all.

She wasn't anywhere near ugly. She had smooth dark skin that I wanted to put my mouth on. I didn't know what it was about her, but whenever I was in her presence, I couldn't stop the nasty thoughts that ran through my head. It was really bad the day she came to give me my phone. Clay and I weren't on the best terms that day either and the next thing I knew, I was fucking Nikki all over the house. I had lost track of time and Clay had come home and caught us in the act. She beat Nikki's ass that day, but she didn't do her dirty like she did at the shop.

I was shocked that she had even put her hands on me. She had never done that before. She fucked my shit up too.

I've never had a black eye before and now I got one because Clay's little ass had a mean ass right hook. Nikki couldn't even walk or anything by the time the ambulance had come. She had to be hauled off on a stretcher. That shit was all fucked up.

I was mad at Brandi for calling the cops on Clay. Yeah, she was putting her hands on me and shit, but I could've handled it. Brandi was scary though. She was always the type of female to call the cops. Brandi had a thing for me too. I could tell by the way she looked at me. Clay could obviously tell too, but I kept telling her that Brandi was nothing to worry about. She wasn't my type anyway. I couldn't fuck with a scary female.

My phone rang, bringing me out of my thoughts that I was having about earlier today. It was my nigga Royal, so I answered it.

"What's good, nigga?" I asked.

"Man, where the fuck you at?"

"I'm at the hospital, why?"

"Me and Kaya just bailed your girl out. You should've been the first mothafucka up there. Not us. If she wasn't done with you before, she probably is now." Damn. I was too worried about making sure Nikki was good and that she wasn't going to press charges, I had forgotten all about Clay. I'm a fucked up nigga.

"Damn, why didn't you call me sooner?" I asked, feeling myself getting a headache.

98

"I didn't know that we were bailing her out. Kaya just told me to take her up there and I didn't ask no questions. Shit, I'm not that type of nigga. She talked shit the whole way until I dropped her ass off. She's done with yo' ass, bruh." I wasn't trying to hear this right now. I knew that I had fucked up, but I didn't want Clay to be done with me at all. I needed her in my life. I really couldn't imagine life without her crazy ass.

"Where did you drop her off at?"

"Your crib."

"Aight, good looking out," I said and ended the call. I needed to get to the house and talk to her. I know that right now, I was probably the last nigga she wanted to talk to, but I was going to try anyway.

"I'll be back up here tomorrow," I told Nikki. She looked at me and rolled her eyes. Well, at least, that's what I thought she did. Her eyes were so damn swollen I couldn't even tell.

"You gotta go see about your bitch?" she asked with an attitude. I didn't know why her ass had an attitude. She knew all about Clay. It wasn't like I was fucking Nikki either. I barely talked to her because after I got caught, I cut her ass off completely. That's why she had just popped up at the shop today.

"Watch your mouth. Try to get some rest, aight?" I hurried out of her room and into my car. I didn't know what was going to happen when I got to the house. I didn't know if she was going to put her hands on me again or what. I just hoped that she was willing to talk to my ass. I had really fucked up… again.

When I pulled up to our house, I didn't see her car in the driveway. I knew that only meant one thing: she was probably spending the night with her mom. I sighed loudly before walking in the house. I wasn't in the mood to be going all the way to her mom's house just to try to talk to her. Her mom couldn't stand me for some reason. No matter what I did, her mom always had a problem with it. It didn't make me no difference though; I wasn't fucking Clay's mom, I was fucking her.

I decided to just get out of the car and call it a night. I would try to go see what was up with Clay tomorrow morning or some shit. It was late right now anyway and they were probably sleeping. I just needed tomorrow to be a better day for me. I needed to cut Nikki off again too. I didn't need to be in contact with her at all. I knew she wasn't going to like that though, but that wasn't my problem.

The next morning, I woke up to my phone ringing. I thought maybe it was Clay calling me, but it was an unknown number. I wasn't going to answer it, but I did anyway.

"Hello?"

"Rome, could you come pick me up from the hospital, please? No one else will answer the phone," Nikki said. Damn, I knew I shouldn't have answered the phone. I should've just let that bitch ring.

"What you mean? Your moms can't come get you?"

"No. She's in Jamaica right now with her boyfriend and my sister's phone is going straight to voicemail."

"Man, aight. I'll be there," I said, then hung up the phone. I really didn't need to be around Nikki at all right now, especially after what happened yesterday, but I wasn't a heartless nigga. I couldn't just leave her ass at the hospital like that. I didn't know how she got my number though. I should probably put her on the block list after I drop her off at home.

It took me about an hour to get ready. I didn't care though. I wasn't in a rush to get Nikki or hear her mouth. I know she was going to have a lot to say about Clay and I wasn't in the mood for it. At the end of the day, Clay was still my fiancé, and I didn't want any bitch disrespecting her. I didn't care who they were. That shit wasn't about to fly with me.

"It took you long enough," Nikki had the nerve to say when I finally made it into her room.

"Shut yo' ass up before I leave you here stranded. I didn't have to come and get you. I was just being nice because I feel bad about what happened yesterday," I let her know as we walked out of the hospital. She didn't say anything back and I was glad. That didn't last long though. As soon as we got in the car, she started talking and wouldn't shut the hell up.

"So, does your little girlfriend know that you came to pick me up from the hospital?" she asked.

"First of all, she's not my little girlfriend. She's my fiancé," I said.

"What? Since when? You really proposed to her?" She sounded shocked and sad at the same time.

"We've been engaged for a little minute now, I just keep fucking up."

"Well, maybe it's not meant for you two to be together then. Ever think about that?" I looked over at her and chuckled.

"Stop saying stupid shit like that. Me and her were meant to be together because that's the only woman I see myself being with and having my kids. No one else." I could tell by the look on Nikki's face that she didn't like the answer that I had given her. I really didn't care, though. That's what she kept failing to realize.

"Wow, really? So what if someone else had feelings for you?"

"There's a lot of bitches that claim they have feelings for me. A lot of them have only had one conversation with me. That don't mean shit, though. The only woman I care about is Clay." She was quiet for a minute, but it didn't last long.

"So what if I told you that I had feelings for you? That still doesn't mean shit to you?" She was really starting to get on my nerves with this twenty-one questions shit.

"Why would you have feelings for me? We only fucked once, then I cut you off because you almost made me lose the best thing that's ever happened to me." She didn't say anything for the rest of the ride. It's about time something shut her ass up.

"I forgot to tell you, I moved," she said once I had pulled up to the apartment building.

"The fuck you mean you moved?"

"I got tired of staying in these apartments, so I moved. I found me a nice little house to stay in," she smiled.

"So you didn't think that was something that I needed to know? You had me waste gas for what? Because you're in your little feelings? Man, where the fuck you live at?" I asked angrily. I was tired of being around her. I know she did this bullshit on purpose.

"I'll put it in the GPS," she said, pulling her cell phone out. I needed to get away from her and fast.

Once she put her address in the GPS, I broke all types of traffic laws trying to get her ass home and out of my car. She was up to some sneaky shit. I could tell just by the way she was acting.

Pulling up to her new home, she quickly got out and came around to the driver's side of the car. She didn't need to do any of this. She was just being extra.

"Thanks for the ride, Rome. I can't wait to see you again," she said.

"You probably won't be seeing me for a while, but aight." She slowly turned to walk away, but not before looking at her neighbor, who was sitting on the porch. That's when I realized that I was in Clay's mom's neighborhood and they were next door neighbors. Clay was sitting on the porch with her mom, staring a hole through Nikki. I felt like I had been set up, but Nikki didn't know that's where her mom lived. Did she?

I knew I was fucked when Clay stood up and started making her way towards Nikki and I. I just knew it was about to be some shit, and there wasn't shit that I could do about it. I just parked my car because there was no way that I could run from this situation like I wanted to.

"Are you fucking serious, Romeo?!" Clay yelled, calling me by my real name. I swear I could see the fire in her eyes and the steam coming from her ears. Nikki had a smirk on her face like this shit was funny. I guess she didn't learn her lesson from yesterday when Clay beat her ass. I quickly got out of my car so that I could stop Clay from getting at Nikki again. Shit, she might kill her this time.

"Clay, chill out," I told her. She didn't even say anything else, she just cocked her hand back as far as it would go, then punched the shit out of me. Once again, my nose started leaking. I really needed to stop underestimating Clay. Her little ass was strong as hell.

"Nigga, you ain't shit! This is where you were all night? This is why you couldn't even call to check on me and make

sure I wasn't in jail anymore?" Clay kept swinging at me and I
was trying my hardest to block her powerful hits.

"That should show you who he really wants to be
with," Nikki said. I didn't even know why she bothered to
open her mouth. Clay stopped hitting me and ran over to
Nikki, knocking her ass out with a two piece. Nikki's face was
still fucked up from yesterday. It looked like Clay was trying
to do some permanent damage.

"Man, chill!" I yelled, holding Clay back.

"Get your hands off of me! I'm done with your stupid
ass! I'm so done!" I just kept holding her, trying to get her to
calm down. She was upset right now and I'm pretty sure she
was just talking out of anger. I hoped like hell she was just
talking out of anger.

She snatched away from me and looked directly into
my eyes. She had tears streaming down her face and that
made me feel even worse than I did. It seemed like she was
crying all the time now and it was mostly because of me.
Damn.

"It's over, Rome. I'm not dealing with this shit
anymore. I need someone who's actually going to appreciate
me and not take me for granted. I'll be by the house later to
get the rest of my things." I could tell by the look in her eyes
that she meant it. That right there was fucking with me. She
couldn't be done with me. She was my everything.

I watched as she walked back to her mom's place. Her
mom's nosey ass was standing on the porch, smoking a

cigarette and shaking her head at us. She was probably about to go in the house and talk shit about me to Clay. I couldn't even bring myself to say anything to her. I wanted to grab her and tell her that she wasn't going anywhere, but my body wouldn't cooperate with me. It's like I was paralyzed. I felt it in my heart that Clay was actually done with me and I couldn't do anything about it. I fucked up again, but this time, I don't think there was any coming back from it.

# Chapter Eleven: Kevin

Amaya was still blowing up my phone like I was her nigga, and that shit was really starting to piss me off. From what Kaya tells me, she's in a full relationship with some nigga, but she's always riding my dick. Literally. I admit that I was still fucking her, but shit, why not? Why give up free pussy if she's constantly throwing it at me?

"It's about time you answered your damn phone! Why the hell do you keep ignoring me? I told you I had something important to tell you!" she yelled once I answered the phone for her goofy ass.

"You said that shit two nights ago when you came over here and all you did was ride my dick and take yo' ass home. Obviously whatever you got to tell me isn't that important," I said, inhaling the blunt that I was smoking.

"Whatever, Kevin. I'm pregnant." I almost choked on my blunt because I was laughing so hard at her.

"What the fuck you telling me for? You better go tell your boyfriend that he needs to get ready to be a full-time dad."

"Kevin, it's not his." I was tired of this conversation already. This is why I don't answer the phone for her. She was always talking nonsense.

"How? I make sure to strap up every time I slide up in you. Don't try to pin that nigga's baby on me because he's not who you want to be with." She was quiet for a little minute and I was about to hang right up.

"It's yours because I poked holes in your condoms."

"Bitch, you did what?!" I know this bitch didn't just say what I thought she said. She wasn't that crazy. She couldn't have been.

"You heard me, Kevin! I poked holes in your condoms, now get ready to be a daddy," she said and ended the call. This bitch had me so fucked up. I knew I should've stopped fucking with her ass a long time ago.

"Nigga, you good?" Royal asked me.

"Man, hell nah. This crazy bitch just called and told me that she was pregnant by me because she's been poking holes in the condoms. I really might go kill this bitch." Royal was laughing hard as hell, but I didn't find anything funny. Nothing about this situation was funny.

"Damn, nigga. You be finding the crazy bitches, I swear." His phone started ringing and I swear this nigga started blushing. What bitch was this nigga talking to that had him smiling like that? That nigga looked like he was in love already. He even walked out of the room so that he could take the call. Lovesick ass nigga.

Rome, on the other hand, was just sitting here looking like he had just lost his best friend. I guess in a sense, he did. Clay came and got all of her shit from her house and bounced. She wasn't even answering any of his phone calls. My man was hurt, and that's exactly why I stayed away from all that relationship shit. I didn't have time for females. All I needed was a quick nut and I was good.

"I'm gonna holla at y'all niggas later. I got some shit to do," Royal said, coming back into the room.

"What bitch you about to go see?" I asked.

"Your sister," Rome said.

"What?" I asked because I was confused.

"He's going to see Kaya. That's why he's been acting like a sprung ass nigga," Rome chuckled. I didn't even know that Kaya was fucking with Royal. Shit, she doesn't tell me about the niggas she fucks with and I prefer to keep it that way.

"Oh, word? You fucking with Kaya? She got you sprung?" I asked, laughing.

"Fuck y'all niggas. I'm not sprung. She's just cool to chill with. But like I said, I got shit to do." Royal dapped Rome and I up then left out of Rome's house. I was about to dip too because I needed to go strangle Amaya's stupid ass. I didn't know if she was really pregnant by me or not, but I hoped she wasn't. I did not want to have a baby by her. She was already crazy. Just imagine how crazy she'll get when she becomes my baby's mother.

"I'm about to go too. Don't sit in here being depressed all night. Go find you some pussy or some shit," I said, standing up.

"Finding some pussy is what got me in this whole situation to begin with. I don't need a new bitch. I need for mine to answer her phone and bring her ass home." I just shook my head at his ass. I never wanted to be like that. I think that may have been one of my worst fears: sulking over a bitch.

After leaving Rome's crib, I was on my way to Amaya. I just had to stop at the gas station first. Before I paid for my gas, I decided to get me a snack because a nigga was hungry as hell, I just didn't feel like stopping anywhere else.

"Excuse me," I heard a soft voice say from behind me. I thought it was going to be some girl trying to get my attention to tell me how good I looked or something. I turned around to look at her and I was in for a big surprise. This girl was gorgeous. I swear she looked like a dark-skinned goddess. Her hair came to the middle of her back and I could tell that it was all hers. Her breasts were an average size, but her ass made up for all of that. That thing was huge and it looked soft as hell. She was wearing a dress that stopped right below her knee and it was making her body look even better.

"I said excuse me. You're standing in front of the chips that I'm trying to get," she said, pulling me out of the daze that she had me in.

"Oh, my bad, ma," I said, stepping out of her way. She didn't even seem interested in me, which was something that I wasn't used to. She just grabbed the chips she wanted and made her way to the back of the store so she could get her something to drink. Without even thinking, I followed her.

"So what's your name?" I asked, standing behind her. She turned around and looked at me. She then smiled at me, showing off her perfect set of teeth.

"Reese."

"You are way too beautiful for me not to have your number." She laughed at me.

"Am I? That's so sweet of you to say. But, I have a boyfriend. Sorry," she said, then walked away. I didn't give a fuck about her having a boyfriend. I just wanted to see what that ass looked like bouncing up and down on my dick. I was hoping that I ran into her again. I was going to make her forget all about her little boyfriend.

Once I finally left the gas station, I was on my way to Amaya's house. For some reason, I thought about Reese the whole time. I didn't know why I was thinking about her like this. I had bitches lined up waiting to fuck me, but I was fascinated with one who didn't even give me the time of day. At least not yet. I couldn't wait to run into her again. I knew that it was bound to happen.

I pulled up in Amaya's driveway and I got mad all over again. I still couldn't believe that she did some grimy shit like this. She must've thought I was a pussy just like whoever her boyfriend was. She was sadly mistaken.

I walked up to Amaya's door and twisted the knob. I was mad as hell that the door was locked. I started banging on her door hard as hell.

"Amaya, open the fuckin' door!" I yelled. A few moments later, the door swung open and there stood Amaya in nothing but a robe. She was looking good as hell right now, but that's not why I was here. She thought what she did was okay and it wasn't. This is why you can't fuck with crazy bitches. I've learned my damn lesson.

"Kevin, what are you doing here?" she asked. She looked shocked as hell to see me. It was probably because she thought what she did was okay and that I wasn't going to be mad about it. Nah, I was beyond mad. I was ready to fight her ass right about now.

"So you think what you said to me on the phone earlier is okay? You think it's cool to walk around and do shit like that?" I yelled, causing her to jump.

"I just want you to love me like I love you! That will finally happen after our baby gets here," her crazy ass had the nerve to say.

"Even if that baby is mine, I still won't love you. All we're doing is fucking. Why the hell you trying to make shit out to be something it's not?" Out of nowhere, she burst into tears. What the fuck?

"You don't understand, Kevin! No one has ever loved me! Not even my own mom!" This is not what I came over here to talk about. I just wanted to know why the hell she was trying to trap my ass. Maybe she wasn't even pregnant. Maybe she just wanted some attention so she made up this bullshit ass lie.

"That doesn't have anything to do with why the hell you poked holes in my fucking condoms!" I yelled, getting frustrated with this conversation.

"I poked holes in the condom so we could be a family and you would love me like I love you. Don't stand here and act like you don't have any feelings for me. I know you do. Otherwise, you wouldn't keep coming back." She thought she knew some shit, but she didn't. I came back because she was always available. I had no feelings for her ass whatsoever. I just wished that she would understand that.

"Your boyfriend doesn't think it's his?"

"No. We don't have sex anymore. He's always too busy fucking other bitches. Me and him aren't even together anymore." She didn't seem sad about that at all.

"Man, how do you even know that you're pregnant? You been to the doctor or some shit?" She started smiling big as hell.

"No, we have an appointment tomorrow. Aren't you excited?"

"Hell no I'm not excited! I don't want this baby. How much does it cost to get rid of the shit?" She twisted her face up like what I said to her was mean or some shit. I really didn't give a fuck right now. If she would've gotten pregnant under different circumstances, then everything would be different. She did this shit on purpose and expected me to be okay with everything.

"Are you serious right now? You want me to get rid of it?" she asked.

"Yep." She started crying again and the shit was pissing me off. I swear she was bipolar as hell. She couldn't be mad at me because I didn't want a baby. We weren't even in a relationship.

"I can't believe you, Kevin. Why don't you care about us? This baby growing inside of me right now is a part of you. Why would you want me to kill it? You want me to kill Kevin Jr?" After she said that, I was done with this conversation. I needed to get away from her because right now, all I could think about was putting my hands on her.

"I'll see you later," I said, turning to leave.

"I'll call you tomorrow so that you can take me to my doctor's appointment," she called from behind me. She sounded happy as hell about that too. I just ignored her ass and kept walking. I was hoping that she wasn't pregnant. If she was pregnant, I was hoping I wasn't the father. I wasn't ready for all of that yet. I don't have a problem with kids at all, but I pictured having kids when I was ready to settle down with someone, and that wasn't happening anytime soon.

When I made it home, my phone was ringing off the hook. It was Brandi calling because she wanted some dick, but I wasn't even in the mood for it. I wasn't in the mood for anything right now. I just wanted to take my ass to sleep and pretend like everything Amaya told me wasn't true at all.

I woke up the next morning to my phone ringing. I should've looked to see who was calling before I answered it, but I didn't.

"Hello?" I said sleepily into the phone.

"Wake up, Kevin. We have a doctor's appointment," Amaya said happily. I sighed loudly into the phone. I didn't want to take her to this appointment because I didn't want it to be true that she was pregnant. If she was pregnant, I was going to be there. I didn't have a dad growing up, so if this child is mine, I don't want them going through the same situation.

"Whatever, man. I'll be over there in a minute." I hung up the phone without waiting for a response from her. I was mad at myself for not being more careful. I should've put my condoms up somewhere she couldn't find them. I still couldn't believe she did this shit. I shook my head and got out of bed. This was going to be a long day. I could feel it.

Before going to pick up Amaya, I stopped at McDonalds so that I could get me something to eat. A nigga was starving and I knew I wasn't going to have time to eat when I got to Amaya's house. I hope her ass had already eaten something because I wasn't buying her shit.

"Funny running into you here. Are you stalking me?" I heard as I waited for my order to get ready. Turning around, I was face to face with Reese's sexy ass. I swear she looked even better than she did the night before. She had her hair up in a bun, and today she was wearing a pair of jeans and a black cut off shirt. She was killing bitches and she wasn't even trying.

"I was in here before you, you're stalking me," I said.

"Boy bye, don't think because you look good I'm about to be following your ass around." She waved me off.

"Don't talk so loud. We wouldn't want your little boyfriend to hear you talking to a real nigga." She started laughing like I had just told the funniest joke.

"I don't have a boyfriend. I just said that because I didn't want to be bothered. I had a rough day yesterday." I wanted to feel some type of way that she lied to me, but I couldn't. I was happy as hell that she was single.

"Word? So you're just a liar?" I asked with a raised eyebrow.

"No, I'm far from a liar. But none of that is important."

"You right. So give me your number and I'm gonna call you tonight." She stood there for a minute like she wasn't sure if she wanted to give me her number or not.

"Alright. Only because I'm in a good mood today." I handed her my phone and she put her number in it.

"I don't even know your name, Mr.," she said smirking.

"Kevin. But you probably won't be calling me that later," I said, winking at her. After that, I got my food and left out of the restaurant. I still wasn't looking forward to this doctor's appointment, but I might as well get it over with.

# Chapter Twelve: Reese

Kevin was probably the sexiest man I had ever laid my eyes on. When I saw him yesterday, I thought I was going to cream my panties by just looking at him. I could already tell what kind of man he was just by looking at him. He probably had bitches lined up trying to get at him. He wasn't going to do anything but shatter my heart into a million pieces because I was going to want something that he wasn't willing to give me.

I was actually shocked to run into him at McDonalds. I wasn't going to say anything to him, but he was looking way too good for me not to. He was everything that I ever wanted in a man. He was tall, probably about 6'3, light skinned, and he had tattoos all over his body. I didn't know why, but I always had a thing for hood niggas. My mom always wanted me to date a white man for some reason. She was always trying to set me up on blind dates with white men, but that's just not what I was attracted to.

My whole life, I've only dated white men. My mom instilled it in my head that a black man would never love me like a white man could. She used to tell me that black men were only good for one thing and one thing only, and that was leaving. My dad had left her when I was a baby and ever since then, she hadn't been the same. All she ever did was talk shit about black men. I didn't understand why when I was younger, but now I knew. She thought these white men would give her what she wanted from my dad, but she was wrong.

My mom had so many boyfriends when I was growing up. It seemed like every month, it was a different man. Of course they were all white. I thought this was normal. I used to do the same thing. Date only white men. It wasn't until I let one of them take my virginity that I knew white men weren't for me. The first time is supposed to hurt, right? Well, I didn't feel a thing. He was moaning more than I was because I wasn't moaning at all. I was disappointed and I didn't understand why my mom thought these white men were so great and they couldn't even please her in the bedroom.

I've only had sex with two people and they were both white. I still keep in contact with one of them because he can make me cum sometimes, but it's not very often. Every single time I have sex with him, I wish it was a black man with at least ten inches of dick. I want a man that will have me walking all crazy the next day. I want to be able to feel him inside of my stomach. I want hair pulling, ass slapping, and choking. I was tired of always doing the same position, which was missionary. That shit got boring as hell fast as hell. I couldn't take it anymore.

After leaving McDonalds, I went straight to my best friend Nikki's house. She had just gotten out of the hospital and I needed to go see her and ask what the hell happened for her to end up in the hospital. I also couldn't wait to tell her about Kevin's sexy ass. He was definitely something to brag about.

When I got to her house, the door was unlocked like always. For some reason, Nikki always kept her door unlocked. Yeah, she lived in a pretty nice neighborhood, but if I were her, my door would stay locked. I don't trust that at all. You never know who might be watching your house, just waiting for the right time to break in.

"Nikki," I sang, walking into her house. "Where are you at, girl?"

"Stop yelling, I'm in my room," she called out. I made my way into her room and I couldn't believe how her face looked. It looked like she had gotten hit by a car or something.

"Goodness, what happened to your face? Are you okay?" I asked, sitting down on the bed next to her.

"Yes, I'm fine as long as I take my pain meds. I got jumped by Rome's girlfriend and some of her hood rat friends," she said, shaking her head.

"What? Why? You don't even talk to that nigga anymore."

"I showed up at his shop and she didn't like that. She has no reason to be mad at me still. She needs to be checking her cheating ass nigga."

"Wait, why did you show up at his shop? Did you tell him that you were going to stop by?"

"I mean, no, but he doesn't ever answer his phone when I call him. I needed to see him so I just popped up." I was feeling bad for Nikki at first, but I wasn't anymore. You don't just show up unannounced like that.

"Of course he doesn't answer when you call. He's trying to work things out with his girlfriend. Nikki, y'all had sex once. You seriously need to let that nigga go. Find you a nigga who doesn't have a girlfriend." She looked at me like I had two heads or something.

"No. I'm in love with Rome and that's who I'm going to be with. I can't help who I fall in love with," she had the nerve to say. I didn't even have anything else to say about this situation. Nikki was on some other shit right now. She knew damn well that Rome will never be with her, but she won't give up.

"Anyway, I met a guy today. His name is Kevin," I said, smiling from ear to ear. Nikki rolled her eyes.

"Girl, I don't care about your white boys. You need a real nigga in your life. You're going to start fucking with Kevin, then come to me complaining about how small his dick is and how you can't feel anything."

"He's not white, bitch. He's black and covered in tattoos. I'm getting wet just thinking about him." Nikki had a shocked look on her face.

"What? You finally came to your senses and found you some dark meat? Oh shit."

"Shut up. He's not dark, he's light skinned. I gave him my number today; I can't wait for him to call me."

"Don't get your feelings hurt. You better make sure he doesn't have any kids or a crazy ass ex. That's something you don't want to get involved with. It's just going to have you looking stupid in the end." I agreed with that one. I didn't have time for some crazy ass ex popping up. I wasn't about to be fighting over any nigga. That wasn't lady like and I didn't want to be out here looking like a hood rat.

I stayed and chatted it up with Nikki for a couple of hours before my phone rang. I got extra excited thinking that it was Kevin calling, but it was just Lucas calling me. He was probably calling for sex and that definitely wasn't happening tonight.

"Hello?" I said, trying not to sound annoyed.

"Hey, beautiful. What are you up to?" he asked, sounding extra happy.

"Nothing. Just over a friend's house."

"Are you free tonight? Do you want to go out to dinner?" I thought about it for a moment. I was free tonight and I could stay out late because I didn't have to work tomorrow. Plus, I was hungry and he was going to be paying. I wasn't looking forward to having sex with him, but I didn't want to pass up a free meal.

"Yes, I'm free, and that sounds like a wonderful idea," I let him know.

"Cool. Do you want to go to Outback? I've had a taste for steak today."

"That's fine."

"I'll be over to pick you up around eight." We ended the call and I rolled my eyes. Lucas was a good man. He was good looking, sweet, and polite. He knew how to really treat a woman, but that's just not what I wanted. I wanted a nigga to demand me to get ready so we can go out. That right there is what gets my pussy wet.

"Going out with your white boy?" Nikki asked.

"Shut up, bitch. I'm not about to pass up a free meal."

"Well, don't call me complaining tomorrow about how terrible his dick was." I ignored what she said and stood up to leave. I needed to find me something to wear. I wasn't going to get all dressed up because I didn't care about looking good for Lucas. Now, if I were going out with Kevin, it would be a whole different story. I said my goodbyes to Nikki and was on my way to my apartment.

I didn't live on the nicest side of town. Believe me, I wanted to, but I couldn't afford it. Working at the front desk of the Marriot wasn't paying me enough. They were paying me enough to be on my own, but I couldn't afford where I really wanted to live. Lucas used to always tell me that once we are official, I can move in with him, but that's not what I wanted. I wanted my own and I didn't want to be in a relationship with him. I wish he could see that, but some people just couldn't take hints.

Once I was inside my apartment, I took a quick shower, straightened my hair, and got dressed in a simple light pink sundress. I didn't care about putting on makeup or anything because Lucas wasn't anyone special. He had seen my bare face plenty of times. As I was adding the finishing touches to my outfit, there was a knock on the door. I sighed and went to go answer it.

"These are for you, my lady," Lucas said, holding a bouquet of red roses. I had told him plenty of times that I didn't like roses, but he still insisted on getting them for me every time he took me out. Roses smelled bad to me and they would make my whole apartment smell bad.

"Thanks, Lucas. You shouldn't have," I said, grabbing the roses. I went to go put them on the counter, then grabbed my purse and was out the door. I hoped this would turn out to be a good night. Maybe he wouldn't want to have sex later.

We got to the restaurant and ordered our food. He was talking so much, telling me about his day and shit. He had been talking about himself since we got here. Not once did he ask if I had a good day or how work was going. I rolled my eyes wishing I would've stayed my ass at home.

"Are you okay? You seem a little off today," he said.

"Yes, I'm fine."

"Are you sure? You know I'm here for you if you need anything." I looked at him and I could tell by the look on his face that he was dead ass serious. My phone started ringing in my purse and I was so glad.

"Hello?" I said without even seeing who was calling first.

"Damn ma, I didn't know you were into white boys," Kevin said. My heart rate sped up. I was jumping for joy on the inside at the fact that he actually called me. I thought he was going to forget about me and call me like two weeks later or something.

"Huh? What are you talking about?"

"Ain't that a white boy sitting in front of you?" I looked around the restaurant because obviously, this man could see me. I didn't see him, though.

"Yes."

"So you like white boys, right?"

"Yes. I mean no. It's just that—" Lucas snatched the phone out of my hand and ended the call. How fucking rude!

"Lucas, what the hell? You saw me having a conversation. Why would you do something like that?" I asked.

"We were having a conversation and what you did was rude. You don't answer the phone while you're at the table with me." I couldn't believe this. He was really trippin' right now. I reached for my phone, but he wouldn't give it back.

"Give me my phone, Lucas. You don't know who it was that I was talking to. That could've been an important call," I said, feeling myself getting upset.

"You can have your phone back after we're done with our meal." I wanted to hit him right now, but instead, I just sat back and didn't say anything else.

"Aye, my man, I believe you have something that doesn't belong to you," I heard a familiar voice say. I looked up to see Kevin's sexy ass grilling the fuck out of Lucas.

"I don't know what you're talking about. Now if you would excuse me, I'm on a date," Lucas said. Oh goodness. Why did he have to say that? This was not a date. I was just here to eat.

"Actually, you know exactly what I'm talking about. I was having a serious conversation with Reese, and you just snatched the phone out of her hand and hung up like I wasn't fucking talkin' or some shit. Now, what I need for you to do is give Reese back her phone because she's already asked you nicely." How the hell did he know all of this? He must've really been watching me the whole time.

"I don't care that Reese was talking to your thug ass. Her and I were having a conversation and you interrupted it like you're doing now." Without warning, Kevin grabbed the back of Lucas' head and slammed it into the table.

"I tried being nice to you, white boy, but you obviously take my kindness for a weakness. Give me the fuckin' phone," Kevin said through gritted teeth. Lucas handed Kevin my phone while holding his nose that was bleeding. I didn't know what to do so I just sat there and watched with my mouth hanging open.

"Let's go," Kevin demanded.

"Huh?" I asked dumbfounded.

"You heard me. Now, let's go." I looked at Lucas one last time before getting up from the table and following behind Kevin. I felt bad as hell for leaving Lucas like that, but it wasn't my fault he was a pussy.

Kevin walked to an all-black Audi. I didn't know what he did for a living, but he had to be getting money if he was driving in this. I had never been in one before. It was even nicer on the inside. I couldn't stop rubbing the leather seats. I didn't even care about what had just happened back at the restaurant. I was just happy to be away from Lucas and even happier that I didn't have to have sex with him tonight.

"Aye, you hear me talking to you?" Kevin asked, pulling me out of my thoughts.

"No, my mind was somewhere else," I honestly told him.

"I said I apologize for handling your boyfriend like that." I chuckled at what he said.

"He is not my boyfriend. He is nowhere close to being my boyfriend. He asked if I wanted to go out to eat and I said yes because I wouldn't have to pay for the meal."

"Right. Whenever you see him again, let him know how rude it is to hang up on people." The fact that Kevin was serious about getting hung up on was a little funny to me.

"I doubt that I will be seeing him again."

"Good. You don't need to be with someone who's a pussy anyway." I didn't say anything else. I was too busy wondering if Kevin had broken Lucas' nose or not.

Kevin pulled up to a nice two story house and parked the car. I didn't have any plans on spending the night with him already. He was probably going to try to have sex with me and I wasn't feeling that at all. I would like to get to know him first before we had sex. Plus, I didn't want him to think I was just some hoe because I gave it up on the first night.

"Who lives here?" I asked, getting out of the car.

"I do." He smiled at me and went to unlock the door. The house was actually really nice on the inside. He couldn't have decorated this by himself. It looked like this was all done by a woman. I was hoping that it was done by his mom or sister or something and not by an ex that used to live here.

Kevin led me to his room that had a big ass bed and TV in it. Even the dressers were large. Now I was really wondering what it was that he did for a living. I hope it wasn't something illegal because I didn't want to be involved in that. I was about to ask Kevin where he worked, but I was stopped because I heard loud ass moaning. Who the hell was in here besides us two?

Kevin heard the moans too, and I could tell by the look on his face that he wasn't happy about them. He quickly walked out of the room.

"Aye, shut the fuck up! Don't nobody wanna hear that shit!" he yelled as he banged on the door. He walked back in the room and he looked disgusted.

"Who is that?" I asked as I sat down on his bed.

"My sister. She lives here too, but I'm starting to see that this is going to be a problem." He came and sat on the bed beside of me.

"So tell me about yourself, Reese." I hated when people said this to me. There wasn't much to know about me at all. I lived a boring ass life. I was a boring ass person.

"I'm twenty-one, I work at the Marriot, and I've never been with a black man before." I regretted the words as soon as they left my mouth. Why the hell did I say that? He didn't need to know that at all. Now he probably thinks I don't like black men and that is clearly not the case.

"What you mean you never been with a black man? What's wrong with us niggas?" he smirked.

"Nothing is wrong with y'all. It's just… It's a long story."

"I ain't got nothing but time," he let me know. I figured that he had a point. I decided to tell him the story about my dad leaving my mom and about her hatred for black men. When I was finished with the story, Kevin was laughing hard as hell. I didn't find anything funny at all, though.

"It's not funny," I said, folding my arms across my chest.

"That shit funny as hell, but now I see why you act the way you do. You just need some black dick in your life." He licked his sexy ass lips, making my panties get wet.

"I'll find out one day," I said, letting him know that he wasn't getting in my pants tonight. I expected him to get upset, but he didn't. He just kicked off his shoes and got comfortable on the bed. We talked about everything. I found out a lot about him and I told him some more about my boring life. I was glad to know that he didn't have a crazy ex or baby mama. Maybe me and him could have a future.

# Chapter Thirteen: Kaya

It had been about a month since I started fucking with Royal. I couldn't believe that this nigga had my head gone like this. I wasn't even hitting up Greg and Mecca anymore. I was spending all of my time with Royal. There was just something about him that I couldn't get enough of. He was like a breath of fresh air.

Royal and I were at the mall because he had no problem spending his money on me. I wasn't complaining either. That just left more money for me to stack in my bank account and use for a rainy day.

"Get whatever you want, but don't take all day like you usually do," he told me as we walked into another store.

"Boy, shut up. Don't be rushing me." I walked away from him so that I could go look at the shoes. I saw some really cute heels online and I just had to have them.

"You know damn well you don't need any more shoes," Royal said, creeping up behind me.

"I do need these. Look how cute they are," I said, holding them up for him to look at them.

"Nah, I don't see it." I shoved it in his face some more because he obviously wasn't seeing how cute these heels were.

"Get that shit outta my face before you get fucked up in here," he said, slapping the shoe away and coming closer to me.

"You ain't gonna do shit." He bit me on my neck and I couldn't help but giggle.

"Royal? I thought that was you," we heard a voice say. He stopped biting on my neck and turned around to see who it was that was talking to him. Of course, it was some female trying to get some attention. You clearly see him all over me, so why would you even try to have a conversation with him?

"Oh, what's up, Zuri?" he said to her. I instantly got mad. I technically didn't have a right to be mad because he and I weren't in a relationship, but we were damn sure acting like it.

"I haven't seen you in so long. I didn't even know that you were in a relationship," she said, eyeballing me like she had a problem. She wasn't anywhere close to being on my level, so I wasn't even going to entertain her.

"Nah, you know I don't do that relationship shit," Royal had the nerve to say. My blood started to boil. I wanted to punch him in the back of the head, but I didn't want to cause a scene in this store.

"Oh really? Well, is your number still the same? If it is, I'll call you later so we can get up like old times," she said smiling. She was happy as hell that he had just told her that he was single. Stupid ass nigga.

"Yeah, it's still the same. Just hit me up whenever." She waved to him one last time before she turned to leave. I wasn't even going to bother asking who the bitch was because there would be no point. I already knew that he would probably be fucking her tonight and that bothered the hell out of me.

"Take me home," I said, putting the shoe down and heading towards the entrance of the store.

"You didn't even get anything," he said, following behind me. I just ignored his ass and kept it moving. I couldn't even believe how this nigga had me in my feelings right now. This had never happened. I never gave a fuck about these niggas, but it was a different story when it came to Royal.

"Girl, you hear me talking to you!" Royal said once we got to the car.

"Nigga, take me the fuck home!" I was so mad right now I could've fought this nigga.

"You better calm that yelling shit the fuck down. I haven't done shit to your ass," he said. I got in the car and slammed the door. I didn't want to be around him at all anymore. For the first time in a long time, my feelings were actually hurt. I even felt like crying, but I wasn't about to do no shit like that. At least not while he was around.

The car ride to my place was quiet as hell. This nigga didn't even have the radio on or the music blasting like he usually did. I didn't care, though. I was just glad that he didn't try to start a conversation with me because I would've ignored him like he wasn't even there. I was beyond happy when we pulled into my driveway.

"Man, what the fuck is wrong with you?" he asked before I got out of the car.

"Nothing. I hope you have fun with Zuri, nigga," I spat.

"That's what you're upset about? Man, I'm not even worried about that girl." I could tell he was lying because he wouldn't even look at me. He had plans on fucking that bitch. I just knew he did because I could feel it. His phone started to ring and he looked at it, but quickly tried to silence it. I just shook my head at him.

"That's the bitch calling right now, isn't it?" I asked. He didn't say anything and that was my answer right there. "Bye, nigga. Don't bother calling me no more. I'm good on your ass," I said and got out of the car before I could say anything else.

"Kaya, you trippin' for no reason!" he yelled out of the window. I ignored him, though. I walked into the house and slammed the door behind me. Fuck him. He wasn't shit anyway.

"Are you okay?" I heard a voice ask me from in the kitchen. I had never seen this girl before. She was pretty as hell, though.

"Yeah, I'm good. I'm just dealing with man problems right now. If you even want to call them that," I said.

"Do you want to talk about it? I'm Reese, by the way. Your brother told me to make myself at home and then he left, so I came down here to make me something to eat." I didn't know why she was explaining herself to me. I would've done the same shit.

"No, you're good. How long have you been messing with Kevin?"

"A couple of weeks now. Most of the time we're at my place instead of here. He said he doesn't want to hear you moaning all night." I was instantly embarrassed after she said that. My embarrassment quickly turned to anger as I thought about Royal going to see that bitch. He was probably on his way right now. I hated that there was nothing that I could do about it because he and I weren't together.

"Well, I'm going to take a nap. I'll talk to you later," I said and made my way into my room. I wanted to call Clay and tell her all about what happened at the mall, but she was still going through it with Rome. She was so depressed now that they weren't together. I hated seeing her like that too.

Just as I was about to doze off, my phone started ringing. I didn't feel like talking to anyone, so I let it go to voicemail. If it was anything important, they'll leave a message or something. That wasn't the case with this, though. They called right back, making me mad. I grabbed the phone and answered it without even seeing who it was first.

"Hello!" I yelled into the phone.

"Damn girl, who pissed in your cereal today?" Mecca asked. I had been ignoring him for like a month now because I was so occupied with Royal. I guess I could start talking to him again.

"I just had a rough day."

"You should come through then. Maybe I could make you feel better." Shit, he didn't have to tell me twice. Plus, Royal is out doing him anyway and I'm single, so why not?

"Okay, I'll be there in a few," I said. We ended the call and I started to get ready. I even packed an overnight bag and everything. I didn't know why I was trippin' over Royal. That nigga would be lucky to have my ass. It's his loss, not mine. There were plenty of niggas that were willing to give me the world. Fuck Royal. I was better off without him anyway.

Once I made it to Mecca's place, he was all over me. He didn't even let me get into the house fully before his lips were all over my neck.

"I missed you, girl. You need to stop holding out on a nigga," he said, removing my clothes. For some reason, I just couldn't get into it. The only thing that was on my mind was Royal. I hated this so much. Every time Mecca would kiss me, I would close my eyes and pretend that it was Royal kissing me instead. Every time he would touch me, I wished that it was Royal's hands instead of his. Don't even get me started on the sex. I had to tell that nigga that he was hurting me just to get him to stop. That nigga wasn't hurting me at all. I couldn't even feel anything since I let Royal slide up in there.

This was just sad. Mecca couldn't even compare to Royal. I should've just stayed my ass at home.

"Damn, you leaving already? We only went one round," Mecca said.

"I know, but I got things to handle tonight." I was lying. I just didn't want to be around him anymore.

"You gonna ignore me for a month again?" I had to keep myself from laughing at his ass. He sounded like a bitch right now.

"You know what, how about you just come with me?" I had plans on hitting a lick tonight because it had been a little minute since I had done that. Usually, I wouldn't do this without my brother, but I'm pretty sure that he was busy. He and I had been slacking. I hadn't even been to the club to work, but that was about to change very soon. I let Royal get in my head and fuck up my money. Never again will I do some dumb shit like that.

"Where are we going?" he said, getting off of the bed.

"To hit a lick." He didn't say anything, but I knew he didn't want any parts of it. That's something else that I didn't like about Mecca. He was a pussy.

"At a house?" he finally asked.

"Yep. Are you coming or not?"

"Yeah. I don't have to touch anything, right?" I chuckled at how scary he was. I bet Royal would do this with no questions asked.

"Sure, if you don't want any money." He was quiet again, but I didn't care. I continued to put on my clothes. I could do this all by myself. I wasn't afraid of anything, so I wasn't even worried.

"If you decide to come, call me, but if not, I'm good." I shrugged my shoulders and left out of his house. I almost called Kevin to tell him what I was about to do, but I decided against it. I could really use him when it came to getting the heavy stuff, but I guess I'll just have to do the best I can without him.

   ***

Night time had rolled around and I still hadn't gotten a call from Mecca, but what could you expect from a pussy? Niggas weren't about shit at all. I stood in the mirror as I pulled my weave into a low ponytail. I was dressed in all black like usual and I was getting more and more excited about doing this. I liked feeling independent, and that's exactly what I was feeling right now. As I was grabbing everything I needed, my phone rang.

"I see you didn't pussy out," I said to Mecca once I answered the phone.

"There ain't no pussy in my blood, Kaya. I'm outside, though." I couldn't help the smile that spread across my face even if I wanted to. I was happy as hell.

"Okay, I'm on the way." I ended the call, grabbed my ski mask and walked out of my room. On the way out, I ran right into Kevin. The look on his face wasn't a pleasant one either.

"Where the fuck you going, Kay?" he asked, looking at the ski mask I had in my hand.

"Nowhere," I lied, not even looking at him.

"Nowhere, huh? Then what you got that in your hand for? Why you dressed in all black? Are you trying to get caught? Or worse, killed? You know you don't do these licks without me, so I don't even know why you're trying." He tried to snatch the mask out of my hand, but I quickly moved before he could grab it.

"I'll be fine, Kevin. I'm not that same sixteen-year-old that you rescued off the streets," I said, walking away before he could say anything else. I wasn't in the mood to hear anything that he had to say. I was doing this without him. He needed to understand that I wasn't a little ass girl anymore.

"You ready?" I asked Mecca once I got in the car. He was wearing all black too. I could see his pistol resting on his lap. For some reason, I felt like he had never used it on anyone. I chuckled to myself at the thought. He was trying to be someone he wasn't. He wasn't about that life and I could tell.

"Yeah, I'm ready." His mouth said one thing, but his body language said something else. This nigga was scared as hell and it was comical to me. I gave him the directions to the neighborhood that I wanted to go to and we rode there the whole way in silence. I didn't have anything to say to his pussy ass and he was probably over there scared for his life. *Pussy ass nigga,* I thought to myself.

"Stop right here. That's the house we're going in," I told him as I pointed to the huge mini mansion across the street. I had been planning on robbing that house for the longest, but every time I told Kevin, he would tell me no and we would do a different house. I didn't understand why he always did that, but I was a little glad he wasn't here right now to tell me no.

"These houses are big as fuck. How do you know that no one is in there?"

"I don't," I said, pulling the mask over my face. He looked at me like he was confused.

"You only brought one of those?" he asked, referring to my ski mask. Oh my goodness.

"I did. I got plenty of them. You should've told me that you didn't have one." He didn't say anything else, he just watched as I loaded my gun, but I could tell he was even more afraid of doing this than he was a few minutes ago. That wasn't my problem, though. I could do this with or without him.

Once I picked the lock to the back door, we were in. This was probably the nicest house that I had been in. There were so many things that I wanted I didn't know where to start. There was a diamond chain with the letter "R" on it and I picked it up. Where have I seen this before? It looked so familiar to me. I shrugged it off and grabbed the PS4, Xbox, and the rest of the jewelry that was on the table. Why did people just leave their jewelry on the table like that? I knew that I was going to get a lot of money just off of the jewelry. I could tell that a man lived here by how it was decorated.

After we got everything, we were out of the house and back into the car. The only thing Mecca touched was the TV that whoever lived there had in the kitchen. Why the hell did you need a TV in your kitchen? What kind of shit was that? I was shocked that he had actually grabbed something, though. I was glad because that was more money for me. I wasn't giving his ass shit. I didn't feel like he deserved it.

"So that's it? No one is going to call the police on us or anything, right?" his paranoid ass asked.

"Boy, shut the hell up. I've been doing this shit since I was sixteen. I know what I'm doing. Stop acting so damn paranoid. That's not a good look on you," I said, playing with the "R" chain. I had seen this chain before, I just couldn't put my finger on where it was that I had seen it. It was really starting to bother me. I guess I wouldn't ever figure out where I saw it at because as soon as the sun came up, I was selling this shit. I couldn't wait to get this money. That's the only thing that made me happy. Not these niggas.

# Chapter Fourteen: Royal

Kaya was really trippin' earlier when we left the mall. She had no right to be mad about anything. Shit, we weren't in a damn relationship so she couldn't be mad about the other bitches that I choose to entertain. I didn't want her to be mad at me, though. When she told me not to call her anymore, it kinda fucked with me. I guess I could've said something once she got out of my car, but my pride wouldn't let me, so I just watched her walk into the house and slam her door.

This is exactly why I don't want to deal with females on no relationship type shit. They're too damn emotional for me. Kaya had me spending my money on her and buying her food all the time and shit. I barely even did that with my ex Paisley. She really had me acting out of character. It was probably for the best that we didn't deal with each other anymore. It was obvious that she wanted more out of this, but she wasn't going to get it. At least not from me anyway.

"I'm so glad you called me back. I thought you were going to ignore me because of the bitch you were with earlier," Zuri said as I sat on her couch. As soon as I left from Kaya's house, I went right to Zuri's. She was a beast at giving head, and I didn't know why I had cut her off in the first place.

"Nah, she ain't nobody," I said.

"Even if she was, she wouldn't be a threat to me." Zuri came closer to me and started kissing all over my neck. "I missed you so much," she whispered in my ear, making my dick hard.

"Show me how much." Zuri wasted no time dropping to her knees and shoving my whole dick in her mouth. I thought my eyes were going to roll into the back of my head when I felt my dick touch her tonsils. Her head should be illegal. I would kill a nigga over this shit.

"Damn, girl," I grunted as I pushed her head further down. I was enjoying the hell out of this. That was until Kaya's face popped into my head. I started to feel bad about what I was doing with Zuri, but I didn't understand why. We were not in a relationship, so I was free to do whatever I wanted. Why did I feel so guilty, though?

"Royal, what the fuck?" Zuri asked. I guess she was feeling some type of way because I wasn't hard anymore. It wasn't my fault, though; Kaya just popped in my head out of nowhere. Now I was feeling like shit.

"My bad. Keep going." She did what I told her to do, but I still couldn't get hard for some reason. This shit was terrible. I could tell that Zuri was getting frustrated and there wasn't anything I could do about it.

"Maybe we should try this some other time," she said, standing up.

"Nah, I'm good. Put that shit back in your mouth."

"What for? You won't even stay hard!" I gave her a look that told her to shut the fuck up and she did just that. Once she had me back in her mouth again, I closed my eyes and imagined that it was Kaya giving me head instead of Zuri. I bricked up instantly. I had to hurry up and fuck this bitch before my shit went limp again.

I pulled Zuri off of me and bent her over the couch. I pulled out a condom that was in my pocket and quickly slid it on, before removing her shorts and forcefully entering her. She cried out, probably in pain, but I didn't care.

"Royal, it's too big!" she yelled. That's why I stopped fucking with her. She couldn't take dick at all. Even if I didn't go hard, she would still end up crying afterward, making me feel like I had raped her ass or some shit. Then, she would blow up my phone begging for it again. That shit got annoying as hell.

I was still imagining that it was Kaya that I was fucking. It was a little hard to do because Zuri's ass wasn't as fat as Kaya's. Her shit was small as hell.

"Yes baby, right there!" she yelled. She was making it hard as hell to think about Kaya because of her annoying ass voice.

"Shut the fuck up," I said. She didn't listen, though. She was still screaming at the top of her lungs and I was starting to get pissed off. I dug my nails into her hips as I forcefully pounded in and out of her. I had to hurry up and finish so that I could leave. I wasn't feeling this shit at all anymore.

"Fuck, Kaya!" I yelled as I filled up the condom.

"Nigga, what? Who the fuck is Kaya?" Zuri yelled. Damn, I didn't even realize I had called her the wrong name.

"Chill with that shit," I said, pulling out of her and making my way to the bathroom. After I had flushed the condom, I pulled out my phone so that I could call Kaya. As soon as I was about to hit the call button, I quickly decided against it. Why the hell did this girl have me trippin' over here like this?

"So you really called me another chick's name and think that shit is cool?" Zuri yelled.

"Man, shut the fuck up! Maybe if you had some good pussy and knew how to take dick, I wouldn't be thinking about other bitches while we fuck!" Zuri looked hurt at what I had said, but I didn't care. She wasn't my bitch and she knew damn well I was fucking other bitches.

"Get out, Royal! I swear you're such an asshole!" she yelled. I shrugged my shoulders and made my way out of her crib. The whole ride to my place, I couldn't stop thinking about Kaya. It was just something about her that was different. I didn't know what it was, but it had me in my feelings. Maybe I just needed to sleep it off. That sounded good to me.

I woke up the next morning later than I wanted to. Usually, I was awakened by Kaya rubbing her ass on me, but I forgot that we weren't fucking with each other anymore. I hadn't been sleeping alone for about a month now, and I had gotten used to it. I liked watching her sleep. Yeah, the shit was weird, but it was fascinating to me.

I sat up in bed and stretched. I thought today would be different and I wouldn't be thinking about Kaya like I was yesterday, but today it was worse. I just wanted to be in her presence. I didn't care about all that fucking shit. That's how I knew I needed to stay away from her. I've never met a female that made me feel like this. This shit didn't even feel right.

Walking down the stairs, I noticed that something was off. I walked into the kitchen and noticed my back door wasn't closed all the way, and the TV that I had in my kitchen was no longer on the wall. I was starting to feel stupid as fuck. No one was stupid enough to rob me because everyone was so damn afraid of me. I wanted to know who was crazy enough to come up in my shit while I was sleeping like this was cool or something. I walked back into the living room and noticed that my PS4 and Xbox were missing too, along with my chains that I had sitting on the table.

"Fuck!" I yelled, kicking the side of the couch. All that shit was just materialistic, and I could easily get it back, but that wasn't the point. It was the principle. Someone was really stupid enough to do this, and I needed to find out who the fuck it was. Picking up my phone, I dialed Rome's number and he answered on the first ring.

"What's good, nigga?" he asked.

"Man, get to my crib, now. We got a situation."

"Aight." After I had ended the call with Rome, I called Kevin and told him to meet me here too. I was mad as hell at myself right now. I never thought to get an alarm system because no one knew where I lived, and I knew no one was stupid enough to try me. I guess I was wrong, though. I sat down on the couch and shook my head. I hoped whoever did this shit was enjoying their last days on earth because it was about to be lights out for them.

"Damn nigga, you knew we were on the way over here. You could've at least put on some clothes first," Kevin said as I let him and Rome into the house. I was in nothing but my boxers, but that's because that's how I sleep.

"Fuck you, nigga. Worry about your outfit, not mine." Kevin waved me off and went to sit on the couch.

"Aye, nigga, what you do with the PS4?" Rome asked, sitting on the couch beside Kevin. I ran my hand down my face and let out a frustrated sigh.

"Somebody robbed my ass last night." They were both looking at me like they didn't believe a word I said. They knew niggas were too afraid of me too, so this shit didn't even sound right coming out of my mouth.

"Fuck you mean somebody robbed you?" Rome asked, looking like he was about ready to fight someone.

"Exactly what I said. I woke up this morning and realized the back door was opened and some of my shit was missing. They took my TV, jewelry, and my game systems. I feel stupid as hell right now." Rome shook his head while Kevin sat there with a weird ass look on his face. I didn't know what that was about, but maybe it was nothing and I was just trippin' or something.

"Who could be stupid enough to rob you? Who even knows where the hell you live at?" Rome asked.

"The hell if I know, but I know one thing. When I find them, it's over for they ass. They fucked with the wrong one today." I was dead ass serious. This shit had me mad as hell. They could've easily killed my ass if they wanted to. I didn't hear shit last night. Most of the time, the slightest sound would wake me up, but I didn't hear anything. Whoever had done this knew exactly what they were doing.

"All of my chains were custom made, so I'll know it when I see it. I doubt the person would be stupid enough to wear them while I'm around, though," I let them know. They both nodded their heads in agreement. It was quiet for a while, but I know they were both thinking about the whole situation. I had never been robbed before, so this shit had me feeling some type of way.

"Damn, this shit is fucked up," Kevin said. I wanted to ask him about Kaya so bad, but I decided to keep my mouth shut. I didn't want those niggas thinking I was sprung or some shit. They would probably clown my ass and I wasn't feeling that shit.

I needed to get Kaya off of my mind, though. There was business that needed to be handled and I couldn't do anything right if I wasn't focused. I'll just occupy myself with bitches I didn't give a fuck about, and maybe I would stop thinking about her ass.

# Chapter Fifteen: Clay

I was so tired of staying with my mom. She had something negative to say about Rome every damn day. I think she was doing the shit on purpose because I got sad every time she brought his name up. Why couldn't she just leave me alone and let me be sad in peace? Who wants to see their daughter sad? I think there's something seriously wrong with my mom. I didn't know what it was, I just knew that I needed to get away from her, and fast.

"Clay, do you hear me talking to you?" my mom said, bringing me back to reality.

"No, I didn't, but I'm pretty sure you're just going to repeat it anyway," I said, rolling my eyes. I didn't mean to come off as rude, but that's what she made me do. I tried to be nice to her, but she pushed my buttons to the point I don't even want to have a regular conversation with her ass.

"I asked when you were going to take that ring off. You two aren't together anymore and there's no reason for you to still be sporting it like you're not single." Once again, I rolled my eyes at her. Why is it any of her concern what I did with my damn ring? It obviously wasn't bothering me, so why did it bother her? She was really getting on my nerves.

"I like my ring and it's fine where it is," I let her know.

"Are you sure about that? How do you know that he's not fucking some random bitch right now? I mean, he did cheat on you once. Then you saw that bitch getting out of his car with your own two eyes." This is exactly what I was talking about. She was always reminding me about the shit that Rome did. It was so annoying.

"He can have sex with whoever he wants to right now because he's a single man. I can't control what he does," I said.

"That's exactly why you need to take that damn ring off. Shit, if I were you, I would go sell it. My ass would've been right at the pawn shop as soon as I saw that bitch get out of his car. Ain't no man gonna make me look like a fool. I don't care how much I love his ass." She shook her head and then picked up a cigarette to light. That's another thing that I was tired of. She was always smoking in the damn house and I hated the smell of cigarettes.

"That's why you're still single, right? Because you don't want a man making you look like a fool? Or is it because you got tired of my daddy always putting his hands on you? You sure did look like a fool to me because you stayed with him for so long." My dad used to beat the shit out of my mom. I used to sit in my room and cry until it was over.

My dad used to only beat my mom when he came home drunk, but that seemed like it was every night for some reason. She would never do anything but lay there until he stopped hitting her. She would always tell me to go to my room so I wouldn't have to see what was going on, though. Just because I couldn't see it, didn't mean I couldn't still hear it. It wasn't until my dad almost beat her to death that she finally decided to leave his ass. She got me and we left in the middle of the night and that was the last time I had ever seen or heard from my dad.

"That was different," she had the nerve to say. I chuckled at her.

"It was? How? At least Rome has never put his hands on me. You can talk shit about him all you want, but he's a better man than that nigga you call my daddy. That nigga you were so in love with." I stood up and made my way into my room. It was time for me to get out of this house. I couldn't deal with her anymore. My phone started vibrating in my hand and it was just another call from Rome. He calls me every day, but I wasn't ready to have a conversation with him. He made me feel stupid as hell and on top of that, I acted out of character because of a bitch that he didn't want to leave alone. Seeing him drop her off had me feeling more stupid than I did before. The look on her face looked like she enjoyed seeing my feelings hurt, so I had to hit her again.

Looking back at the whole situation, I wish I would've just walked out of the tattoo shop instead of hitting that girl. Yeah, she deserved to get hit because her hands shouldn't have been on my man at all, but it wasn't worth going to jail. Now that I think about it, I should go pay Brandi's snitching ass a visit. I didn't like her already and her calling the police on me made me want to beat her ass even more. I don't think fighting her is worth it, though.

My phone rang again, ending my thoughts of hurting Brandi, and I decided to answer it. He couldn't possibly be that desperate to talk to me.

"Hello?" I said into the phone, obviously annoyed.

"Damn bae, why it take you so long to answer your phone for me? Don't tell me you're still mad at the shit that happened with Nikki." I couldn't believe he had the nerve to even ask that. He shouldn't even say that hoe's name around me.

"Are you serious right now? Why wouldn't I still be mad about you and your girlfriend?" I asked, feeling myself getting angry. I knew I shouldn't have answered the damn phone. I should've kept ignoring him like I'd been doing.

"I'm sorry. How many times do I have to tell you that? Why can't you just come back to the house so that we can talk this out? You know I don't like you being away from me for too long." I had to admit, hearing Rome's voice had me wanting to crawl back to his ass. I missed the hell out of him, but every time I thought of him, I thought about him cheating on me with that Nikki bitch.

"I'm not ready to talk to you yet, Rome. Maybe some other time," I said. I knew damn well if I met up with him somewhere to talk to him, I would go right back to his ass and I don't think he would learn his lesson.

"You trippin', Clay. Shit ain't the same without you here. I need you beside me at night." I was quiet for a minute because I honestly didn't have anything to say right now. Why did he have to do this right now? Or a better question is, why didn't he understand that what he had done had really hurt me? This is exactly why I needed to stay away from him.

"You don't even realize how bad what you did really is. What if I was driving around with a nigga I cheated on you with? How would you feel?" I asked.

"Shit, I'd kill you and him."

"Exactly my point. Don't forget that I walked in on the bitch with her hands all over you and you had the nerve to have your eyes closed like you were really enjoying that shit. Then, on top of that, my ass ended up in jail because of you and you didn't even try to come bail me out. Yeah, I know that I told you not to, but you could've come. Instead, you go see about that stupid bitch at the hospital." I shook my head because just thinking about this whole situation was pissing me off. There had to be something still going on with those two. He was acting like it was.

"I know I fucked up, Clay. Why can't we just move past this shit?" I started laughing at his stupid ass. He really thought he could give me a fucked up apology and I would just come running back to his ass? No, it didn't work like that.

"Are you still fucking that bitch, Rome?"

"No, I'm not still fucking her. I hadn't even talked to the girl until the day she came to my shop." For some reason,

I just didn't believe him. I couldn't believe him. His actions were showing me that he was still in contact with the hoe. It didn't seem like she had just popped up on his ass.

"Yeah, whatever, Rome. I'll talk to you when you stop lying to me." I hurried and ended the call before he could say anything else. This whole situation was stressing me out. I just wish that Rome would've never cheated on me. We wouldn't even be going through this and I could be at home sleeping in his arms every night.

"He is probably on his way to fuck another bitch as we speak," my mom said, standing in my doorway. Of course she had been listening to my whole conversation. I just ignored her and dialed Kaya's number. They had enough rooms in their house, so I'm sure they would let me stay with them.

"Hello?" Kaya said into the phone. She didn't sound like herself. She sounded sad as hell.

"Kaya? Are you okay?"

"Yes, I'm fine." I could tell she was lying, but I wasn't going to press the issue. If she wanted to tell me, then she would, but I wasn't going to force her to tell me something she didn't want to.

"Can I come crash at your house for a couple of days? I can't take staying with my mom anymore." I heard my mom smack her lips, but I really didn't care. I didn't want to be around her anymore because all she was doing was making me feel worse than I already did.

"Of course you can come stay here. You can stay as long as you want."

"Thank you so much. I'll be over there in a few." As soon as we got off of the phone, I quickly got off of my bed and started packing a few things that I would need. My mom was still standing there just staring at me, but I was ignoring her ass. She and I needed our space. I didn't know why she always acted like this when it came to Rome, but it was starting to get old. She needed to find her a man and worry about what hers is doing instead of always being in my relationship.

When I was finished getting my things together, I walked right past my mom without even saying anything to her. Just like I expected, she followed right behind me. I knew she was about to start talking shit and I wished she would just leave me alone.

"So, how long are you going to be jumping from house to house because of this nigga?" she asked once I put my bag in the backseat.

"As long as I want." I didn't even look at her when I said that. I just got in the driver's side of my car and started it up. I was so over my mom. Maybe she would be better when I came back to visit. I didn't plan on coming back here at all. My mom had serious issues that she needed to deal with.

I had planned on going straight to Kaya's house, but I drove past a bar, so I decided to stop and get me something to drink. It had been a little minute since I actually went out and enjoyed myself, so why not do it now? I was just going to get me a couple of shots, then I would be on my way.

It seemed like as soon as I sat down at the bar, all of the niggas wanted to be in my face. I didn't come here for that. I came here to get me something to drink and enjoy myself. How can I do that with all of these niggas all over me?

"I'm not interested," I said, waving them all off. I ordered three shots of Hennessy, but before I could pay for them, someone from behind me said,

"I got it." I rolled my eyes. I didn't need a nigga paying for shit. I had it. Clearly, I wouldn't even be sitting here if I couldn't pay for my own shit.

"I could've paid for that myself," I said with an attitude. He sat down beside me and chuckled.

"I figured that, but I felt like you were way too beautiful for me not to offer to pay."

"Nigga, you didn't offer to pay. You did pay. You handed the bartender a fifty-dollar bill."

"Is that a problem?" I finally looked up at him and he was gorgeous. He looked a little too good. He was light skinned with long dreads that came past his shoulders, and he had tattoos everywhere. He even had a couple on his face. Most of the time when I see face tattoos, I immediately get turned off, but everything about him was turning me on. He smiled at me, showing all the gold in his mouth and I felt myself getting hot. No man had ever had this effect on me other than Rome.

"No, it's not a problem," I quickly said, then took a shot. I needed him to go away. Technically, I was still in a relationship and I was sporting this big ass engagement ring. I didn't need to be entertaining a nigga.

"So what's your name, gorgeous?" All these compliments he was giving me wasn't helping at all. I looked down and blushed.

"Clay. What's yours?"

"Raymond." He didn't look like his name would be Raymond. I didn't have anything else to say, so I took another shot. He put his hand on my thigh, which caught me completely off guard. I hate to admit it, but everything he was doing was getting me hot and bothered. I needed to get myself together and get away from him. He was really trying to get me in trouble.

"You got about two seconds to remove your hand from my girl's thigh before I blow your brains out, my nigga." I knew that voice all too well. This couldn't be happening right now. I closed my eyes and opened them, but he was still standing there with a gun to Raymond's head.

"Rome—" I started, but he cut me off.

"Shut the hell up, Clay," he demanded. I closed my mouth without hesitation. Raymond didn't look afraid at all. This crazy ass nigga actually had a smirk on his face. What the fuck was that about?

"What's up, little brother? You not happy to see me?" Raymond asked. Little brother? I never knew that Rome had

161

siblings. I had met his family plenty of times and they never even brought up another brother.

"Fuck you, nigga. The fuck you doing here? And why the hell you all up in my girl's face like you ain't got no damn sense."

"Shit, she didn't tell me she had a nigga." Damn. Why did he have to go and say that stupid shit? He was trying to get both of us killed.

"She didn't have to, nigga. You see that big ass ring on her finger. You knew exactly who she was when you approached her. So give me a reason I shouldn't kill your ass right here." Rome still had the gun aimed at Raymond's head and everyone in the bar was staring at us. I was pretty sure that someone had already called the police. I needed to get Rome out of here and fast. I couldn't have him going to jail over no stupid shit like this.

"Rome, stop it. You're going to end up in jail. There are too many people around for you to be doing this shit," I said, getting off the bar stool and walking over to him. He looked down at me, then back at Raymond. I guess what I said worked because he put his gun up.

"Let's go," he said to me.

"I drove myself here," I let him know. I didn't want to go anywhere with him. I guess he forgot that we were still on bad terms.

"Damn, your bitch doesn't even want to go with you," Raymond said laughing. I was starting not to like his ass.

Rome hit his ass with a right hook that sent him flying out of his chair. That nigga wasn't laughing anymore. He then grabbed my arm and led me out of the bar.

"Why the fuck were you smiling all up in that nigga's face like you're not in a damn relationship?" Rome yelled once we were outside. I wasn't in the mood for this at all. Me and Raymond were doing nothing but having a conversation.

"I wasn't smiling in nobody's face! Now let me go so I can leave!" I yelled back. If he thought I was coming home with him, then he had another thing coming.

"Nah, you're coming with me," he calmly said, then opened the passenger side door.

"No, I'm not. I came here to get a drink, then go to Kaya's house. Those plans didn't include you in them at all. How the hell did you even know where I was at anyway?" He laughed, but it was more of an annoyed laugh. Not a happy laugh.

"You should stop questioning me and get your ass in the car before I push you in. I've done it before and you know damn well I will gladly do it again." I didn't say anything else. It was obvious that Rome wasn't about to sit here and take "no" for an answer, so I just got my ass in the car before he started acting a fool out here. He slammed the door shut behind me. He then walked over to the driver's side and got in. I already knew that it was about to be a long night. The only thing is, I wasn't mentally prepared for it.

# Chapter Sixteen: Kaya

I closed my eyes and opened them again, hoping that this would all go away. I was really hoping that it was a bad dream that I couldn't wake up from, but when I did wake up, everything would go back to normal. Once I opened my eyes again, I knew that I wasn't dreaming and this shit was real.

Staring at the two positive pregnancy tests, I didn't know how to feel. How the hell did I let this shit happen? I was so damn stupid for this. I knew for a fact that I was pregnant by Royal because we never used protection. Shit, the first night we had sex, he didn't wear a condom. I didn't think about it until the next day, so I took one of the Plan-B pills. I guess it was pointless to take one of those pills and still let that nigga fuck me raw. I sat down on the toilet, not knowing what to do next.

Should I keep it or should I get rid of it? Royal and I weren't meant to be together because he doesn't do relationships and neither do I. I enjoy my single life, doing whatever I want, and not having to answer to anyone. Adding a baby to that just didn't fit at all. I didn't want to tell Royal because he would probably think I'm just one of those females that's trying to get him to stay by pinning a baby on him. That wasn't me at all.

I couldn't keep this damn child. I just couldn't. There was money that needed to be made and all this baby would do is slow me down. At the same time, I actually wanted to keep it. Was that weird? The thought of having a baby that was half of me and half of Royal made me feel warm on the inside. Especially if I was having a little girl.

"What the hell you doing in there?" Mecca asked, banging on the door. He wanted to have sex, but I couldn't have sex with him knowing that I was pregnant with another man's baby. Even though I didn't plan on keeping it, I still wouldn't feel right doing that shit.

"I'll be out in a minute, nigga, damn," I said. I knew something was wrong. I hadn't been feeling like myself for the past couple of days and I had been feeling very emotional. Almost everything had my ass ready to start crying. When my period didn't come, I knew something was definitely wrong. I went right to the drugstore and got a box of pregnancy tests. Now I was sitting here feeling stupid.

I finally got off of the toilet and threw everything away. I didn't want Mecca to know that I was pregnant because he would probably get all excited and think the baby was his and beg me to keep it. I didn't plan on telling anyone until after I got an abortion. I'm calling the clinic first thing in the morning. I just hoped that I wouldn't regret my decision down the line because my mind was made up. I couldn't keep this baby. It would cause too many problems in my life.

"I gotta go," I said to Mecca as I walked out of his bathroom.

"Damn, already? We haven't even done shit yet." He was sitting on his bed with his shirt off, looking good as hell, but I had other things on my mind right now. No, I had Royal on my mind right now. I hate not talking to him every day. He didn't care though because not once has he called just to talk like we used to do. I wanted to just say fuck him and move on with my life, but I couldn't. I thought about this man all day and all night. When I'm having sex with Mecca, Royal is the one I'm thinking about.

"Yeah, I got some things to take care of." He looked at me like he knew I was lying, but I didn't care. He would be alright. As I was walking towards the door, I felt a sharp pain in my back. I didn't know what it was, but I couldn't move.

"You on your period or some shit? Why the hell you bleeding?" Mecca asked, walking towards me. I knew exactly what that meant.

"Take me to the hospital and call my brother!"

\*\*\*

For some reason, when the doctors told me I had miscarried, I was sad as hell. I didn't understand why though because I had planned on getting rid of the baby anyway. I didn't know what was wrong with me right now. Mecca had been by my side the whole time, but I guess he was in his feelings now because I told him the baby wasn't his. He would get over it, though.

"Kaya, what the fuck happened?" Kevin asked as he came into the room. For some reason, I didn't want to tell him that I was pregnant and had lost the baby. I felt like he would be mad at me. It was really weird, but I was feeling like a little kid right about now.

"She was pregnant and lost the baby," Mecca said since I wouldn't say anything. I grilled him and so did Kevin.

"Who the fuck are you?" Kevin asked with the nastiest look on his face.

"Mecca. She was at my house when the whole thing happened." Right now, I wished he would just shut the hell up.

"Oh, so you were the daddy?"

"No, Royal was," I said before Mecca could say anything else. Kevin didn't look too happy about what I had told him, but I didn't understand why. That's when I noticed Royal standing by the door. Royal and I locked eyes and he was looking sad as hell too.

"Can I have a moment with her?" he asked, looking directly at Mecca. Mecca's pussy ass wasted no time standing up and leaving the room. Kevin walked out right behind him.

"Why didn't you tell me you were pregnant?" he asked, walking over to the hospital bed.

"I had just found out literally minutes before this bullshit happened. I wasn't planning on keeping it no way, so you didn't have to worry about me pinning a baby on you."

"What the fuck you mean you didn't plan on keeping it? What kinda shit is that?" I didn't expect him to get so mad when I said that. Shit, I thought that he would be happy about me not wanting to keep the baby. He didn't want a relationship with anyone, so why the hell would he want a baby? This nigga was backwards as hell.

"There was no point of keeping it. You were doing your own thing and I was doing mine. Why complicate things with a baby?" I shrugged.

"That's some real fucked up shit to say. It probably was for the best that we stopped fucking with each other." I swear hearing him say that shit hurt worse than losing this fucking baby. Out of nowhere, the tears started falling. This was too much. Everything was too much right now.

"Man, chill with that crying shit," he said, walking closer to me. That's when I saw the exact same chain that I had taken the other day from that house. It had the "R" on it and everything. The only difference was this chain was gold and the other one was silver. Oh shit. I had robbed Royal. That's why Kevin wouldn't ever want to rob that house when I would bring it up. That nigga knew who lived there. I felt myself getting hot. Did he know that I did it? Was he looking for the people that did it? I hope he's not really here because he wants to kill me.

"Aye, you hear me talking to you?" he asked.

"No, my mind was somewhere else," I said and wiped my tears.

"I said I was sorry for saying that shit to you just now. I need to be comforting you, not making you feel worse than you already do." I don't think he had a clue who robbed him. If he did, he was doing a really good job of acting like he didn't know that it was me.

"It's fine," I said, looking away from him.

"You miss me?" he asked, catching me completely off guard.

"What?"

"You heard what I said, Kaya." I did hear exactly what he said, I just didn't want to answer his question.

"Yes," I said, barely above a whisper.

"I miss your little ass too." I couldn't help but smile after he said that. I thought he didn't give a fuck about me anymore and that he was done with me.

"Really?"

"Yes, really. I can't stop thinking about your ass for some reason. You're different from these other bitches that I've been fucking with. I see us going somewhere." He bit down on his bottom lip like he didn't mean to say what he had said. He makes the same face when he's fucking me from behind. I closed my eyes and squeezed my legs together because I was thinking about him fucking me now. Shit, I wish we could do it right now. He was looking good as hell, like always, in his Nike sweat suit. I don't think he could ever look bad. Every time I saw him, my kitty instantly got wet. This man just didn't know what he did to me.

"Open your damn eyes and listen to what I got to say," he demanded. I opened my eyes and looked at him. He looked like he was in deep thought. "So who is that nigga out there?" I chuckled because I knew he felt some type of way about Mecca.

"He's a friend, why?"

"You fuckin' that nigga?"

"Why is that any of your concern?" I raised an eyebrow at him.

"Because you're mine now. Tell that nigga he can go kick rocks because whatever y'all had is over." I didn't have anything else to say because I was stuck on the fact that this nigga had just really made me his girlfriend. He didn't ask how I felt about it or anything. To be honest, I was happy as hell. I wasn't the relationship type, but if he was willing to give things a try, I guess I could too.

"Okay," I said smiling. I could drop Mecca in a heartbeat. Shit, his dick didn't have shit on Royal's anyway. "You need to drop all your hoes too. I don't have a problem cutting a bitch," I let him know. He chuckled but didn't say anything. This nigga must not know that I was being serious. I was dead ass serious.

## Two Weeks Later

I was back dancing at the club every night again, and Royal hated the idea. The first day I went back, he didn't really have too much to say about it, but now it was a whole different story. This nigga argued with me up until I left for work, then his ass would show up at the club mad as hell. He really didn't have anything to worry about. As long as he kept dicking me down like he was doing, then I wasn't even looking at any other nigga. The only thing these other niggas were good for was throwing money my way.

"Where the hell you think you going in that little ass dress?" Royal asked as I stood in the mirror and straightened my hair.

"You know exactly where I'm going. Don't even start this shit," I said. I knew that he was about to start telling me how I don't need to be down at the club and that he doesn't like how all of these other men are basically seeing everything that belongs to him and bullshit like that. I wasn't trying to hear it today.

"Man, why the fuck you still going to that club every night? Why can't you just let me take care of you? Shit, I make enough money for the both of us."

"Boy, shut up. I don't want you to take care of me because I can do it myself. I like making my own money. I've been doing it for a long time now. I won't feel right sitting on my ass all day not doing shit but spending your money."

"That's some bullshit. Could you at least find a different type of job?" I finished straightening my hair, then walked over to where he was sitting and kissed him on his cheek.

"Who am I leaving the club with every night? You, right? You have nothing to worry about, okay?" He still didn't look happy. He looked like what I said made him even more upset.

"Fuck all that shit. You're not going to be dancing at that club for too much longer. I put that shit on my life." I didn't even say anything back to him because there was no point. That would just start an argument and that's something that I was trying to avoid tonight.

For some reason, I just wasn't feeling tonight. As soon as I got to the club, I was ready to turn back around and go home. I thought about doing just that, but there was money to be made. I would take off tomorrow or something. There was no point of leaving since I was already here.

"Girl, I hope Royal's fine ass comes in here tonight. He's been in here every night, but never wants a dance from me," this stripper named Roxy said to her little friends as we all sat in the locker room getting ready. Hearing her talk about Royal had me ready to beat her ass. I was glad she said he never wanted a dance from her. The only ass that would be bouncing on his lap tonight or any other night was mine.

"Shit, fuck that dancing shit. I'm trying to take that nigga home with me," her friend Red said.

"You and me both, bitch." They high-fived one another and I was trying my hardest to keep my cool. I didn't want to end up fighting one of these hoes and end up getting fired from dancing at the club.

"Roxy, let me talk to you for a minute," I said. Roxy and I were never really fans of each other. It was really her because I didn't care about her at all. As soon as I started dancing at the club, she started hating because she wasn't getting all of the attention anymore. That wasn't my problem, though. I was still getting paid regardless.

"Yeah?" she asked when she made it over to me.

"I would greatly appreciate it if you wouldn't talk about Royal. He and I are a thing now so you need to find someone else to lust over." I didn't even look at her when I said that. I continued to put my makeup on in the mirror.

"You and Royal are a thing? Yeah right, I'll believe it when I see it." She laughed like something was funny and I got pissed off.

"This is your only warning, bitch. Don't act surprised when you get your ass beat." She really took what I said lightly. I hated when bitches underestimated me, but it was okay; I could show these bitches better than I could tell them.

# Chapter Seventeen: Reese

Since I had been spending all of my time with Kevin, I felt it was only right that he met my mom. He agreed with it and he actually wanted to meet her, the only thing was, my mom had never met a man I was dating that was black and not white. Then on top of that, Kevin wasn't one of the black men that acted white. He had no problems letting his hood side show, and I was afraid of how my mom would react to that.

"Are you ready?" Kevin asked me. He had basically moved in with me at my apartment. I felt a lot safer with him being there. He just made things so much better.

"Yes, I'm ready. I hope she likes you," I said.

"She probably will. Women always seem to like me, but I don't blame them. Look at me." I hit him in his arm and tried to walk away, but he grabbed my arm and pulled me close to his body. He smelled so damn good. He always smelled good, though.

"Don't be like that, you know I'm only playing." He kissed me on my lips then we were on our way out the door. Kevin and I haven't had sex yet, and I was thinking that tonight might be the night that I finally make that happen. I didn't want to have sex with him all early, then he starts thinking that I'm a hoe or something. I also wanted to make sure he actually liked me and he wasn't just trying to get into my pants. He's proved to me that he's not trying to do that and I was really thankful for that. I planned on being real nasty tonight, only because it would be my first time having sex with a black man. I was praying that I wouldn't be disappointed.

When we pulled up to Red Lobster, I got nervous all over again. When I talked to my mom over the phone, I didn't tell her that Kevin was black. Hopefully, that wouldn't make a difference, though. I guess Kevin could sense that I was nervous because he grabbed my hand and gave it a little squeeze.

"Chill, she's gonna love me," he smiled. I sure hope she does. There's no telling what might come out of my mom's mouth once she sees us. I checked myself in the mirror one last time before I got out of the car, and Kevin was right behind me. We walked hand in hand into the restaurant, and I spotted my mom immediately. She was always early. I don't think there was ever a time that my mom was late in her life.

"Hey, mom," I said as we approached the table. She smiled at me and stood up to give me a hug.

"Hey, baby, you look so good." She kissed me on my cheek, then we all sat down.

"This is Kevin, the one that I was telling you so much about." My mom's smile instantly faded when she looked at him. I knew it was only going to go downhill from here. Her eyes scanned his tattoo covered arms and she twisted her face up. Oh gosh.

"Well, he's a lot darker than what I'm used to seeing you with," she said. Kevin chuckled and smiled at her.

"It's nice to meet you, Miss."

"Karen. My name is Karen. So, Reese, where did you find him at?" I didn't like how she was acting like he wasn't human just because he was black. How could someone who shared the same dark chocolate skin as me, not like black men? Or black people period for that matter. She only hung out with white women too. That's the weirdest thing I've ever heard.

"Kevin and I met at a gas station, then we ran into each other the next day at McDonalds," I told her smiling. I was so glad that I ran into him. He's really making my life worth living for.

"Mhm, I see. Are you a lawyer, Kendrick?" my mom asked him. I tried my hardest not to roll my eyes at her because she got his name wrong on purpose. She was being very petty and it was getting on my damn nerves.

"No, I'm not a lawyer. I'm working on opening up my own barbershops, though," he said. I knew what Kevin did for a living. He and I had already had this conversation. At first, I didn't like the idea of him robbing people for a living, but I feel like it's better than selling drugs. I supported him one hundred percent with his barbershop ideas.

"I figured you weren't a lawyer. No one is going to hire you with all that mess on your arms. I don't understand why black men are always doing that to themselves," she said, shaking her head. My mouth fell open. I couldn't believe she had just said that. Then, Kevin was just sitting there like none of the things she was saying was bothering him at all. I didn't understand it at all.

"Mom, that was unnecessary," I said.

"No, all of the tattoos that he has are unnecessary." I bit my bottom lip because I really wanted to cuss her out right now. She had no right to be acting like this towards him. He has been nothing but respectful to her and she was doing this bullshit.

"Why are you acting like this? He has done nothing to you."

"I'm sorry that I'm not a big fan of your thug boyfriend, Reese. I'm not going to sit here and pretend that I like him when I don't." I could see that my mom's words were starting to get to him by the way he was clenching his jaw. It was probably best if we left.

"You know what, I'll talk to you later, mom," I said, getting out of the booth. Kevin stood up and was right behind me. I'm glad he didn't lose his cool and cuss her out. I wouldn't have been mad at him at all because she really deserved it. She had no reason to be that rude to him.

"So this is why you haven't been answering your phone all day? Because you're too busy out entertaining another bitch!" I heard someone yell from behind us. I turned around to see some female approaching Kevin and I. Who the hell was this chick?

"Man, Amaya, go on with that shit," Kevin said. The fact that he knew who she was made me instantly mad.

"No! I sit at home all day every day waiting for you to return my phone calls and you never do! This is not how you treat the girl who is carrying your baby!" she yelled. By now, everyone in the restaurant was staring at us, including my mom. She was shaking her head at us.

"Chill with that shit. I don't know whose baby you're carrying!" Kevin yelled back. I felt my heart rate speed up. He has a baby on the way? I asked him if he had a crazy girlfriend or baby mama and he said no. He lied right to my face. Now here I was standing here looking like a complete fool.

"You know damn well this is your child! You weren't denying it last week when we were at the doctor! You were bragging about how your son is in there, right? Or do you not remember that because your little bitch is standing right there?" I didn't even have anything to say. My feelings were so hurt. It felt like my heart had literally been ripped out of my chest. I didn't even want to stay to hear the rest of the conversation, so I just walked out of the building. As soon as I got outside, I realized that Kevin had driven us here and I didn't have a way back home. This just wasn't my day at all.

I sat down on the bench and grabbed my phone from out of my purse. I guess I would just call an Uber and go back to my apartment. I was not about to ride in the same car as Kevin. There's no telling what might happen. I might end up putting my hands on him and causing us to crash, then we'll both be dead. It's best if I stay away from him right now.

"Reese," I heard Kevin yell. He was walking towards me with that bitch right behind him, still yelling. I didn't have time for this type of drama. I was a quiet girl that didn't mess with anyone. I didn't like bringing unwanted attention to myself when I was out in public.

"Leave me alone, Kevin. Take your bitch and just leave," I said.

"Man, fuck her! She's not who I want, you are. Come on so we can go." I looked up at him and laughed. Why the hell would I go anywhere with his lying ass?

"Fuck me? It wasn't fuck me when I was sucking your dick last week!" the girl yelled. It seemed like everything that came out of her mouth wasn't doing anything but making me feel worse than I already did. Now it all made sense as to why Kevin wasn't pressuring me to have sex with him. He was still fucking that bitch. I shook my head as I tried to keep the tears from falling. I didn't want them to see me cry. Fuck both of them.

"Bye, Kevin. It was fun while it lasted. I don't want to be the one that breaks up a happy family. I'll drop all the things that you have at my apartment off later," I said, wishing the Uber would hurry up and get here.

"Are you serious right now?" he had the nerve to ask. Why the hell wouldn't I be serious? What sense did that make?

"Yes. I am very serious. I wish you the best." Kevin stood there for a minute before he finally decided to walk off. His little bitch was right behind him, still talking shit. She was annoying as hell. I was glad that I didn't have to deal with her.

"That's why I didn't like him. Those thug types always come with a lot of drama. That's why you should stick to white men. You don't need to be out here arguing about a no-good ass man anyway. What happened to that other guy you were seeing?" my mom asked, sitting on the bench beside me. She was talking about Ethan, but I didn't care to talk to her right now. I didn't even want to be around her. I just wanted to go home and cry.

I thought Kevin was different. I thought he and I would actually have a future. I especially thought he would rock my world with that dick of his, but I guess that's what I get for thinking. That's what I get for getting my hopes up. I guess I'm just going to stay single for the rest of my life because I didn't want a white man. That's just not what I was attracted to anymore.

"Thanks, mom, but I don't want to talk about it right now," I said.

"I understand. Now you see why I don't deal with those kind of men. It's a lesson learned for you." She patted my thigh, then she stood up to leave. I felt so stupid right now. I couldn't wait to tell Nikki what happened. I knew she would probably make me feel better. She was always good at doing that.

Once I finally made it home, I got out of the Uber and made my way up the stairs to my apartment. I was surprised as hell to see Kevin waiting by my door for me. I'm glad I didn't give him a key or anything because he would be in my apartment and I didn't even want to deal with him right now.

"Why are you here, Kevin? Shouldn't you be making sure your baby mama is good?" I asked.

"Fuck that bitch. She's not my baby mama. Are you going to let me explain this or what?" He had the nerve to have an attitude. The only person who should have a damn attitude is me! This nigga embarrassed me in front of a lot of people. One of those people being my mom!

"There's nothing to explain, Kevin. You lied, now I'm done. It's simple as that."

"I didn't lie about shit, Reese." he said. I rolled my eyes at him.

"You remember when I asked if you had a crazy girlfriend or baby mama? Your answer was no, right? You could've told me right then that there was a girl you might have gotten pregnant, but you didn't. You just lied to my face. I guess you didn't expect her to pop up on you, huh? Well, I'm glad she did. Now I know not to even waste my time with you anymore." Kevin looked sad as hell after I said that.

"But, Reese—" he started, but I cut him off.

"Save it for the next bitch 'cause I'm done." I unlocked my door and walked into my apartment, quickly locking the door behind me. I knew Kevin would try to walk in right behind me and I didn't want to deal with him right now. I wanted him to leave me alone and go on with his life. I didn't have time to be with a man who was a liar.

I plopped down on the couch and turned on the TV. I was sad as hell. I had so many things planned out for Kevin and me, and now none of that would happen because he was a liar and he was about to be a dad. I wasn't going to play step-mommy to anyone's child. Plus, from the way his baby mama was acting at Red Lobster, she probably wouldn't want me around her child anyway.

I pulled out my phone so that I could call Nikki. Her face had healed finally, and she wasn't embarrassed to be seen in public anymore. Maybe I should tell her to come over here because I really didn't feel like driving.

"Hey, bitch, it's about time you called and checked on your best friend," she answered. She and I hadn't talked in a couple of weeks because I was so busy with Kevin.

"Shut up, the phone works two ways. You haven't called to check up on me either," I laughed.

"I know, I've been busy plotting on how I'm going to get Rome to get me pregnant." I could tell by the tone of her voice that she was dead serious. There was something really wrong with my friend. Why couldn't she see that Rome didn't want her? He was never leaving his girlfriend for her, even I could see that.

"You need to leave that man alone, Nikki. You might end up getting hurt again and this time, it might be worse. You never know," I said.

"Well, I love him and I'm not going to give up on him," she said, sounding stupid as hell. I decided to just ignore her and let her do her own thing.

"Do you have anything planned for tonight?"

"Nope. I was just going to sit here and watch movies by my lonesome."

"Good. Come to my place and do that with me. I don't want to be alone tonight."

"Oh, so when Kevin doesn't have time for you, that's when you decide to hit me up and want my company." I rolled my eyes.

"Fuck Kevin." I didn't even want to think about him right now. I didn't want to think about him at all anymore.

"What done happened? Y'all break up?" I chuckled at her because he and I weren't together. I was hoping that we would be, but I guess the universe had other plans.

"I'll tell you when you get here. Bring the snacks too."

"Whatever, bitch, I'm on the way."

About an hour later, Nikki and I were sitting on the couch watching old movies and eating ice cream out of the bucket. I had gotten a few text messages from Kevin, but I didn't even bother to look at them or respond. He wasn't getting it for some reason. I was done with him. I wasn't about to be a fool for anyone.

"So did the bitch have a belly yet? Do you think she was really pregnant?" Nikki asked after I told her what went down today at Red Lobster.

"At first, I didn't want to believe that she was pregnant, but once he started denying the baby, I knew for a fact that she was pregnant. She even said he went with her to the doctor's appointments. He wants it to be a boy." I shook my head, getting mad about the whole situation all over again. I knew he was too good to be true.

"I can't stand niggas like that. He's probably been leading her on, and now that she's pregnant, he wants to act like he doesn't want shit to do with her. I swear I wish Rome would've gotten me pregnant. I would make his little girlfriend's life a living hell."

"Either way, I'm done with him. I don't need that kind of drama in my life. Maybe my mom was right, I should just stick to the white men." Nikki rolled her eyes at me.

"You better not go back to those lame ass white men who think they're better than everyone. All you need to do is find you a black man who can lay the pipe. After that, you'll be wondering why the hell you were fucking with a white man in the first place." I couldn't help but laugh at what she had said. She was probably right, though. I just didn't want to waste my time on someone again. I wanted the next man I entertain to be on the same page as me. I'm too old to be playing these childish ass games. I just wished Kevin would've been the one I settled down with. It hasn't even been a full day, and I was already missing him. I already knew that it was going to be hard for me to move on, but as long as he stayed away from me, then I would be good. I hope.

## Chapter Eighteen: Kevin

Mad isn't even the word to describe how I was feeling right now. I was livid. I could just strangle Amaya. The only thing stopping me from doing that is the fact that she's pregnant. I still don't believe it's my child. I knew I should've just cut her ass off until she had the baby and I was able to get a DNA test.

"Why you over there looking so mad? You upset because I ran your little girlfriend off?" she asked smiling. I was sitting in her apartment on the couch, trying to get Reese to answer my phone calls and text messages. She really wasn't fucking with me at all. I know that Amaya's house is the last place that I should be right now, but I had to come over here to let her know that she's fucking with the wrong one.

"Man, shut the fuck up before you make me do some shit that I regret," I spat. She had a smirk on her face like she was enjoying all of this shit and it was pissing me off even more.

"Boy bye, you ain't gonna do shit. I don't know why you were out with the bitch anyway like you don't have a woman," she said with an eye roll.

"A woman? Amaya, you're not my woman. The sooner you realize that, the better off you'll be. I don't want to be with you. Shit, I don't even want you to suck my dick anymore. You fucked up the best thing that's ever happened to me because you wanted to be childish. Now, ask yourself this; why the hell would I want you after that?" She had the nerve to look sad after I said that, but that shit wasn't moving me at all. Amaya fucked shit up for me. Reese was someone who I could actually see myself settling down with. She was everything that I wanted in a woman, plus more. Amaya just had to come and fuck that shit up for me, though.

"You don't mean that shit," she said.

"That's your damn problem, Amaya! You always thinking that I don't mean something when I do! I'm sitting here telling you that I don't want to be with your crazy ass and you think I don't mean it! What the fuck is wrong with you?"

"You don't mean it! You told me that we were going to be a family!" I massaged my temples because I felt a headache coming on. I've never said no shit like that to her before. I don't know what the hell is going on in her head, but it's definitely something wrong with her ass.

"When the fuck did I say that shit? Refresh my memory because I don't remember that at all." She smacked her lips and got off the couch to go into the kitchen. I followed right behind her ass. I could tell she wasn't taking this conversation seriously and that shit was pissing me off too.

"If she was pregnant, would you act like you didn't want her too?" she asked, getting a water out of the refrigerator.

"Nope. She and I would be a family," I said without even thinking. Amaya's mouth fell open.

"What's so good about her? Why can't you do the same with me?" She had tears in her eyes and I really wasn't in the mood for her theatrics.

"Well for one, she didn't have a boyfriend when I met her. She's not fucking the next nigga while she's with someone else because she actually has morals. Two, I know for a fact she wouldn't do no grimy shit like poking holes in my condoms, and three, she's not crazy like you. You have a serious issue. You might need to go get that shit checked out." Amaya didn't say anything. She just looked at me with so much hatred in her eyes. She then opened the water bottle that she had and threw it in my face. I was mad as hell, but the only thing that I could do was laugh.

"Man, I'm gone. Don't hit me up until after you have the baby," I said, turning to leave.

"Wait, Kevin! Don't leave! I'm sorry, I just don't like it when you call me crazy." I ignored her ass and kept walking. I was serious about her not hitting me up until the baby was born. I didn't have time for her. I needed to get Reese back too. I didn't know why she had me in my feelings like this. She and I weren't even in a relationship. Then, on top of that, we hadn't even had sex yet. This girl really had my head gone.

I got in my car and just sat there for a minute, not wanting to go home. I didn't want to go there and hear Royal and my sister fucking because he's always over there. It seems like that's all they do and that shit is annoying as hell. That nigga might as well move in and give me his damn house.

I decided to go and see what that nigga Rome was up to. I guess Clay and him were back together, so we haven't really been seeing much of him. He's too busy trying to make sure she doesn't leave his ass again, but I don't blame him. If Reese ever gives me another chance, I'm not fucking up ever again. I don't like the way I'm feeling right now, so I'm going to try my best to make sure she never wants to leave a nigga again.

Pulling up to Rome's crib, I spotted Clay sitting outside on the porch, smoking a blunt. That's something that I usually didn't see at all. Clay wasn't the type to smoke. She would drink all day long, but you would never see her smoke anything, not even cigarettes. I got out of my car and walked up to the porch.

"What's good big head? Why you out here looking all stressed and shit?" I asked.

"Because niggas ain't shit," she said, shaking her head. I knew she was talking about Rome, so I didn't ask anything else about it. I didn't want to be out here while she talked shit about my nigga. That shit didn't seem right to me.

"He in the house?" I asked, changing the subject.

"Yep. His bitch ass is in there." I just laughed and walked into the house. She must really be in her feelings for her to call him out his name like that. Rome was sitting on the couch, looking depressed as hell. What the hell did these two have going on now?

"Why the hell you and your girl looking all depressed and shit?" I asked, sitting down on the couch beside him.

"Man, shit is all fucked up right now. She doesn't trust me for shit. She always thinks I'm lying about some shit when I'm not. Then on top of that, she thinks I'm still talking to Nikki behind her back." He had a bottle of Hennessy in his hand, drinking it straight out the bottle.

"Well, she did catch that bitch getting out of your car. Then on top of that, you went to see Nikki in the hospital and didn't even check on Clay with the whole jail situation. You keep giving her reasons not to trust you," I let him know.

"No the fuck I'm not. I've been with her ass 24/7. Then when I leave to go to the store or some shit, she's asking if I went to go see Nikki. The shit is annoying as hell. Why doesn't she understand that she's the only woman I want?"

"Because you cheated, nigga. That's not some shit that she's gonna just forget."

"Well, she needs to. This not trusting me shit is starting to get old fast as hell." Rome didn't understand that what he did was wrong as fuck. He didn't understand that Clay's feelings were still hurt from when he cheated, then all the shit

191

that he's done for Nikki just made everything worse. He just thought she was going to get over it and they were going to move on and live happily ever after. It didn't work like that, though. He had a while before things went back to normal in their relationship.

"I'm having female problems too," I said after a moment of silence.

"With that bad ass dark skinned bitch?"

"Reese. Her name is Reese," I let him know. I didn't like how he just called her a bitch like that. He knew damn well that if I called his girl a bitch, he'd be ready to box.

"Oh, my bad, nigga. What happened with y'all?"

"She took me to meet her rude ass mama today and Amaya popped up telling Reese that she was pregnant by me and shit, so now she doesn't want anything to do with me. I planned on making things official between us after today, but she's not even fucking with me no more." Rome started laughing like I had said something funny just now. Nothing that I said was funny and this nigga was over here dying like I had just told the funniest damn joke.

"Nigga, you always talking about me looking all sad and shit when I'm having problems with my lady, now you're the one looking like a sick damn puppy." He laughed some more and the shit still wasn't funny to me.

"Fuck you, nigga. This shit ain't funny. I didn't even get to fuck yet." His laughter stopped immediately after I said that.

192

"Damn nigga. How you sprung and you haven't even fucked yet?"

"Fuck you, nigga. I'm not talking to you about my female problems no more," I said. Him laughing had me feeling some type of way. This was not a laughing matter. I had to find a way to get Reese back in my good graces. I just didn't know how to do it.

The next morning, I was up bright and early because I planned on going down to Reese's job. I called and texted her all last night, but they all went unanswered. I was starting to get annoyed with all of this shit. While I was blowing Reese's phone up, Amaya was blowing mine up. I didn't know what was wrong with her. She just couldn't take rejection. I was starting to regret the day I started fucking with her.

I was hoping that there wasn't a lot of people at her job yet since it was still so early. I just needed her to talk to me, but I didn't think I could wait until she was on her lunch break. It was killing me that I wasn't able to talk to her all night like we usually do. I couldn't even sleep last night because I didn't have anyone to cuddle with. She has really made an impact in my life in a short period of time.

I sat in my car outside of her job, trying to get my thoughts together. In all honesty, I didn't know what I was going to say to Reese when I saw her. I didn't know how she was going to react to seeing me either. I hope she didn't try to get me put out. I would hate to have to fight those security guards, but I would, just to talk to Reese. Getting out of my car, I slowly made my way to the entrance of the hotel. Her shift had just started, so there weren't many people in here. I was beyond happy about that.

Seeing Reese sitting at the front desk had my feelings everywhere. She was looking good as hell in a simple pair of denim jeans and her work shirt. Her long black hair was pulled up into a messy bun, and the only makeup she had on was some lip gloss. Her lips were looking so soft, I wanted to suck on them. She was too busy typing on her computer to notice me walking towards the front desk.

"You look even more beautiful at work than you do at home," I said, leaning against the counter. She looked up at me and rolled her eyes. Something that I expected. I was prepared for her attitude.

"Kevin, what the hell are you doing here?" She didn't sound like she missed me at all last night. Damn, was she really done fucking with me?

"We need to talk. I'm tired of you ignoring me like we're some fucking teenagers or some shit. That shit is dead as fuck." I gave her a look that let her know that I wasn't playing. She sighed and stopped typing on her computer.

"Talk," she demanded.

"Look, I know I messed up with that whole Amaya situation, and I should've told you about her, but I didn't. I don't know why I didn't tell you that there's a possibility that she might be carrying my child. I guess it was because I don't want it to be true and I can't stand that bitch. The only girl

I'm worried about is you. I had a terrible ass day yesterday without you. Stop treating a nigga like this." I felt like I was begging for her to talk to me, but right now, I would do anything to get her back. She started giggling and I didn't know what she found funny.

"You're so cute when you're trying to apologize," she smiled.

"I'm not trying to be cute, girl, I'm being serious." She bit down on her bottom lip, making my dick instantly hard. I wanted to be inside of her bad as hell right now.

"Okay, Kevin, you only get this one pass because we aren't in a relationship, so I really can't be upset with you. This is the only pass you get, though so don't fuck anything else up," she said, pointing her small finger at me. I couldn't help but smile at her. She didn't even know that she had just made me the happiest man on earth.

"Will you get in trouble for going to the bathroom?" I asked.

"No, I can have bathroom breaks, silly."

"Go to the bathroom. Right now." She slowly got up from her chair and made her way to the bathroom. I followed right behind her, ready to be inside of her. She didn't even know what she was getting herself into right now.

"We can't be in here for too long, Kevin. I'm not trying to lose my job," she said once I had her in the last stall. I didn't even respond back to her. I forcefully kissed her, sticking my tongue down her throat. She let out a quiet moan and my dick was begging to be released.

Once I had her pants off, I pushed her onto the wall and entered her from behind. Slowly sliding inside of her, I felt like I had died and went to heaven. I had never been in some pussy that felt this good. She felt virgin tight and I had to think about other things so that I wouldn't bust too quick.

"Oh my… Kevinnnn!" Reese yelled out as I slowly pumped in and out of her. Her moans were like music to my ears.

"Damn girl," I grunted, biting my bottom lip. Had I known that she was going to feel this good, I would've been slid up in her. She was coating my dick with all of her juices and the sight alone had me on the verge of cumming.

"Don't stoppp! I'm gonna cum!" she yelled right before she started squeezing my dick with her pussy muscles. Once she did that, I couldn't control myself anymore. I released all inside of her, not even caring that I wasn't wearing a condom. She had me in here moaning like I was a little bitch. That shit was crazy because this had never happened to me before. I slowly pulled out of her because I didn't want to be out of that little piece of heaven that I had just experienced, but she had to get back to work and I needed a nap after this.

"I can't believe I just let you do that," she said, wiping herself off with some toilet tissue.

"Yeah, but you loved it just as much as I did." She slid her pants back on and fixed her hair.

"Shut up. You just need to be ready for round two when I get off." She came closer to me and kissed me. I couldn't be happier right now. Having Reese back made me feel like a new man. I was determined to never let her ass get away again. This was the start of something great. I could feel it.

# Chapter Nineteen: Kaya

"Wake that ass up," I heard Royal say. I was trying my hardest to ignore him and finish getting my beauty sleep, but he wasn't having that. I feel soft kisses starting from my lower back and leading up to my neck, which he knew was one of my spots.

"Mmm," I moaned with my eyes still closed. He stopped kissing me and slapped me hard on my ass.

"Get up, girl. I know the dick don't have you that tired." I finally sat up and folded my arms across my chest. I was not a morning person at all. Especially since I was still working those late hours at the club. Why couldn't he just let me sleep? He was being so inconsiderate right now.

"Royal, take your ass on somewhere. I'm tired as hell and you wanna wake me up all early and shit," I said with an obvious attitude.

"Be quiet and go put some clothes on. You don't want to spend the day with your man? Damn Kay, that's fucked up." He put his hand on his chest like I had really hurt him. He was so damn sexy, I couldn't even be mad at him. He was standing there looking like a sexy ass chocolate bar. Damn, no wonder my ass had gotten pregnant the first time. I couldn't keep my hands off of him even if I wanted to.

"Where are we even going first of all? And how do you even know that I want to go with you?" I asked, watching him get his clothes and stuff together.

"My crib. I can't take staying the night here every night. Shit, I miss my bed. Plus, whoever your brother's new girl is was moaning all loud last night. I don't want to hear that shit. Now I know how he feels when you be moaning extra loud 'cause you can't take the dick."

"I can take it!" I yelled. Yeah, he was working with a monster, but I knew how to handle it now. At first, I couldn't take it. I had never had something so big before, but now, I was a pro. Sometimes, I was even out fucking Royal. That's something that I thought would never happen because that nigga was like the damn energizer bunny.

"Don't be mad. I know what I'm working with, so it's okay that you can't take it sometimes." He got back on the bed and kissed me. He only did that because he knew damn well I was about to start arguing with his ass. His kisses always made me weak. We could be arguing about something serious as hell, but as soon as his lips met mine, I forgot what the hell I was even mad about. That was the case right now too. The only thing I was thinking about was how wet I was getting just from this kiss. I moaned into his mouth and he pulled away.

"Get your horny ass up so we can go. Once we get to my place, I'll give you all the dick that you can take." He kissed me on my forehead and got off the bed. I hated when he did shit like that. He knew exactly what he was doing to me. That's why he was wearing that stupid ass grin on his face. I couldn't stand him sometimes.

I rolled my eyes and got off the bed so I could go get in the shower. I locked the door behind me so that Royal wouldn't come into the bathroom. He always wanted to be in the bathroom while I was in the shower because he liked watching me, but since he wanted to hold out on the dick until we got to his house, I wasn't going to let him in the bathroom.

"Kaya, why the hell you got the door locked? Open the door so I can come in!" Royal yelled from the other side of the door. I smiled at myself and turned on the water.

"Sorry, I can't hear you! I'm in the shower!" I yelled back. I couldn't help but laugh at myself for being so damn petty, but I didn't care right now. I got in the shower and I made sure it was a long one, just to keep Royal waiting since he wanted to wake me up out of my sleep.

After my shower, I wrapped my large towel around my body and made my way back into the room. Royal was sitting on the bed looking annoyed as hell and I still didn't care. I had to admit, I was excited about going to his house because I had never been before. Well, in his mind I had never been before. I was just glad that he was actually inviting me. We were always here at my home and it didn't bother me that he never invited me to his home. Now that I was thinking about it, I did want to move away from Kevin. We had been living together since I was basically sixteen and it was time to move on.

"Hurry your slow ass up. I'm tired of waiting for you. I'm about to leave yo' ass," Royal said as I was putting lotion all over my body. I knew he only said that because he was horny as hell. I could see the lust in his eyes as I slowly rubbed up and down my legs. Oh, and the bulge in his pants was almost impossible to miss. He wanted me just as bad as I wanted him right now. He was just being childish.

Once I was finished putting the lotion on, I put on some denim shorts and one of Royal's black t-shirts. I loved wearing his shirts. They always smelled just like him no matter how many times I washed them. When he would be out handling business and I would be missing him something terrible, I would smell one of his shirts and feel a lot better.

"Hold on, I gotta straighten my hair," I said, plugging my flat iron up. Royal got off of the bed and unplugged my flat iron. He then grabbed my cell phone and purse and pushed me out of the room. He was so impatient.

"I'm tired of waiting for your slow ass. Go get your ass in the car," he demanded. I liked when he talked to me like that. For some reason, it always turned me on. I smiled at him and made my way to the car. I was actually excited about going to his house. I bet it was huge. I was already thinking of ways I could decorate and add my touch to it.

"I don't know what the fuck you smiling so hard for. I'm not even fucking with you right now," Royal said once he got in the car. He was just mad because I took my time getting ready. He would be my friend again as soon as we made it to his house and I dropped my pants. He couldn't keep his hands off of me, especially when I was naked.

"Shut up, you know you can't get enough of me." I smiled, then kissed him on his cheek. He didn't say anything else. He just started the car and we were on our way to his place. I could barely contain the excitement that I was feeling right now.

For some reason, when we got to the neighborhood that Rome lived in, I started to get nervous. What if this all was a set up? What if he knew that I robbed him, and he's bringing me to his house so he can kill me or something? I didn't understand why Royal never said anything about it though. He never told me that he had gotten robbed or anything. It's almost like he didn't care about it. He was too calm about the whole situation. If someone robbed me, I'd be ready to find whoever did it and murder them.

"Kaya, you alright?" Royal asked, pulling me out of my thoughts.

"Yeah, I'm good. I'm just a little hungry," I lied. I wasn't hungry at all. My appetite was completely gone. I didn't even want to be around Royal right now.

"Well, I hope you can cook, 'cause I'm hungry as shit too. Come on so I can give you a tour of the house," he said, getting out of the car. I slowly followed behind him. The house was beautiful. It looked like one of those houses that would be featured in a magazine. Being that the sun was up, I could actually see better. Downstairs looked the same. He still hadn't replaced his game systems that I had stolen or the TV that was in the kitchen. I still didn't understand why the hell he needed to have a TV in the kitchen, but he did.

"I had a TV in here, but some fuck niggas robbed my ass some weeks ago and now the shit is gone. Just wait till I find the dumb ass niggas that did this shit. It's lights out for their asses," he said. I swallowed hard and didn't say anything. I just hoped that he wouldn't find out that it was me. Maybe I could somehow frame Mecca so Royal will think it was just him that did it. I didn't care too much for Mecca anyway, so it wouldn't be that hard.

"Girl, where the hell is your head at today? I keep trying to have a conversation with your big head ass and you're not even listening," Royal said. I looked at him and he had an annoyed look on his face.

"I'm sorry. What were you saying?"

"I'm hungry and ain't shit to eat here. Let's go out to eat." He didn't have to tell me twice. I wanted to get out of this house anyway. It was making me feel paranoid as hell. I almost ran out the door and to his car. He didn't think anything of it though. He just thought I was hungry as hell. I needed to be away from his house. I still couldn't believe this was happening right now.

Royal ended up taking me to this Mexican restaurant called La Parrilla. I had never been here before, but I've heard many people talk about how good they were. I loved Mexican food, so I was probably going to enjoy the food regardless.

"Let me ask you something, do you ever think about the baby we lost?" he asked once we were seated. This question caught me completely off guard. This was something I didn't think he wanted to talk about, so I just kept everything to myself. Clay still doesn't even know about the miscarriage.

"Yeah, I think about it every day," I honestly replied. I always thought about my child that I would never get to meet. When I was alone, I thought about it a lot. I wanted it to be a little girl so that I could love her like my mom didn't love me. I wanted to dress her up, put pretty bows in her hair, and make sure she wouldn't want for anything. I would shower her with kisses each and every day so she would know that she was loved by me. I wanted her to know that she would always be loved by me.

"How do you feel about it? I've noticed that when something is bothering you, you like to keep it to yourself. That's not a good thing, Kay. You should be able to talk about your problems, especially with your man," he said, looking at me.

"I'm sad about the whole thing still. I only knew I was pregnant for a couple of minutes and then the next minute, I was losing the baby. I know I said that I didn't plan on keeping it, but now I'm not so sure if that would've been the case." I shrugged my shoulders. I really didn't want to have this conversation right now because it was starting to make me sad.

"Oh yeah, you were going to keep my seed. Whether you liked it or not. You got me fucked up thinking you were going to kill my child like that." I could tell that he was still feeling some type of way about me wanting to have an abortion. Looking back at the whole situation, I couldn't even believe that I even thought about killing my child. How could I kill something that was a part of me?

"Yeah, I sometimes wish that I was still pregnant though. I didn't even get to hear her heartbeat or anything. I didn't get to feel her little kicks; shit, I didn't even get to experience morning sickness. Everything just happened so fast." I shook my head and before I knew it, the tears were falling faster than I could catch them. I didn't want to cry right now. Especially in front of Royal. I felt embarrassed as hell right now. Royal got up and came to my side of the table. He wiped my tears and hugged me. He kissed me on my forehead and told me that everything was going to be okay. This was the side of Royal that I wasn't used to, but I loved it. He was making me feel a lot better and all he was doing was hugging me.

"Hey, Kaya, I haven't seen you in a minute," I heard a familiar voice say. Looking up, I saw Erica looking at Royal and I like she had a problem. I rolled my eyes because I didn't even know why she came over here to speak to me.

"Hey, Erica," I said dryly.

"Is this your nigga for the week? How much is he paying you?" See how this bitch was trying my life right now? She came over here trying to start shit. She should've just stayed where the hell she was at.

"Nope. This is my boyfriend. You remember, the dude from the restaurant that wouldn't dare chase me because he had so many other options?" I smiled at her. By the look on her face, I could tell she didn't like the answer I had given her.

"Oh, well y'all cute or whatever. I'm here with my boyfriend," she said, looking directly at Royal like he was supposed to feel some type of way that she had a boyfriend or something. It was obvious the she and Royal knew each other. I think that's the real reason she brought her annoying ass over here. It's like she was trying to rub the fact that she had a boyfriend in Royal's face and he couldn't care less, like me. I still had yet to meet the nigga that beats her ass, but I didn't care about that either. Shit, she wasn't my damn friend.

"Oh, you are? Well, maybe you should go back to the table with him. I'm sure he wouldn't like the fact that you are all the way over here in my man's face," I said, starting to get annoyed. Right after I said that, Mecca walked over to the table. What the hell? Why couldn't Royal and I just eat our food in peace?

Mecca looked like he was about ready to kill Royal, but we all know his pussy ass wasn't about shit. I guess he was still feeling some type of way that I cut him off for Royal, but he'll be alright.

"This is my boyfriend, Mecca. Mecca, this is my friend, Kaya." I could tell by him walking over to us that she was afraid of him. This couldn't be true. I know Erica wasn't letting Mecca's scary ass put his hands on her. This shit was so funny. I tried to hold my laugh in, but it came out anyway. It wasn't a small snicker either. I was laughing loud as hell. I was laughing so loud that the people in the restaurant were starting to look at me. Even Royal was looking at me like I was crazy.

"This is your boyfriend? This has been your boyfriend the whole time?" I asked once I had my laughter under control. She folded her arms across her flat chest.

"Yes. Is there a problem?" She had an attitude now, but I honestly didn't give a fuck. She shouldn't have brought her ass over here to my table.

"Nope, there's no problem at all. It was good seeing you, Erica. Mecca," I said, dismissing both of them. All I wanted to do was enjoy my meal with my man and they were making it hard for me to do that. They were still standing there looking stupid as hell. They were acting like they didn't understand what the hell I had just said.

"Did you not hear my girl or something? She just dismissed the both of you. Why the hell y'all still standing there looking stupid?" Royal spoke up. Erica looked hurt. She really was looking like her feelings were hurt and I didn't understand why. Mecca mugged Royal and Royal mugged his ass right back. I was so happy when they turned to walk away. They were killing my vibe.

"How do you know Erica?" I asked once they were back at their table.

"What makes you think I know that bitch?" he asked with a raised eyebrow.

"Nigga, don't think I'm stupid. Erica and I are not cool like that. She only came over here because of you. I know how females work." He chuckled.

"I fucked her maybe once or twice. I think. I don't really remember. I know she has a mean head game though." I didn't know why, but for some reason, I felt some type of way after he said that. I knew I shouldn't care because I know that it happened in the past, but I couldn't help the way I felt.

"Oh," was all I said. I didn't even want to have this conversation anymore.

"What you got an attitude for? You're the one who asked. Since we're asking questions, what the hell was she talking about when she asked how much I'm paying you? Paying you for what?" Damn, I was hoping that he didn't catch that. Boy, was I wrong.

"How much you're paying me for sex," I said. When I first started getting money after I fucked niggas, I never felt bad about it. I had to make my money somehow, and it was only two dudes that I was fucking for money. Now looking at Royal, I felt dirty as hell. I didn't even want to tell him that I did that.

"You fuck niggas for money?" I could tell that he was obviously bothered by what I had just revealed to him. I mean, who wouldn't be? That's not something you want to find out that your girlfriend was doing before y'all got together.

"Yeah. I had it hard growing up, so I had to do what I had to do." Royal was quiet for a minute before he started nodding his head.

"You ready to go?" he asked. He was acting like he didn't want to be around me at all anymore. I should've just kept my mouth shut.

"Umm, yeah. I guess so." Royal threw down a fifty-dollar bill and walked off without even waiting for me. I knew he was mad, but how could he be mad about something that happened in the past? He had a past just like I did. He shouldn't let this bother him at all.

The whole car ride he didn't say a word to me. He didn't even turn on the radio. It was an awkward silence and him ignoring me was really starting to hurt my feelings. What really sealed the deal was when he pulled up to my house instead of his. Why the hell were we back here?

"Why did you take me here? I thought we were chilling at your place today." I said, looking at him.

"Nah, I got some business to handle. I'll hit you up later though," he said without even looking at me. I couldn't believe this shit. He had no reason to be mad at me right now. I didn't say anything though. I just got out of his car and walked to the front door. Royal backed out of the driveway and sped down the street before I even got in the house. He didn't even wait to see if I had made it in the house safely. My feelings were really hurt right now. Royal had never acted like this towards me before. I didn't know why, but for some reason, I felt like everything was going to get worse from here.

# Chapter Twenty: Clay

I woke up in bed alone to the smell of breakfast. That was something that didn't happen very often. It was always me cooking breakfast for Rome's ass, not the other way around. I threw the covers off of me and made my way down the stairs. The TV was on, but there was no one watching it. Rome knew I hated when he did that, but he still did it anyway. It was annoying as hell. I went to turn the TV off, then I made my way into the kitchen where Rome was.

The table was filled with food. It looked like Rome had cooked a meal for a whole football team. Rome was standing at the stove in nothing but his basketball shorts. He looked good enough to eat from behind. It was crazy. He turned around because I guess he felt my presence.

"Good morning, beautiful. I made you breakfast," he smiled. I couldn't help but smile back at him. These last couple of weeks things have been going really bad for us. All we do is argue. We don't even have makeup sex afterward. It's been so long since I've had some dick so my attitude has been all fucked up.

"Yeah, I see. You think you made enough?"

"I had to make sure I made everything that you liked so that you can have options." He pulled me closer to him and gave me a kiss. Something that we haven't done in weeks.

Since I was sexually frustrated, the kiss had me horny as hell. I was just about ready to say fuck the food and have him for breakfast. He pulled away and led me to the table. There was so much food, I didn't know where to start.

"You didn't have to do all of this, Rome. You know I have no problem cooking breakfast for you," I let him know.

"I know that I didn't have to do it, but I wanted to. I know I've been fucking up a lot lately, and acting like I don't appreciate you, so I wanted to do something for you to show you that I still care. You mean the world to me and I don't know what I would do without you." I didn't expect this at all. Rome wasn't the type to put his feelings out like this, so the fact that he was trying was enough for me.

"I know I may have made you feel like you weren't the number one lady in my life, but I'm letting you know now that you are. You're the best thing that's ever happened to me and I'm letting you know now that you need to start planning the wedding. I don't know how you're going to feel about having a big belly and walking down the aisle either," he said smirking. I looked at him like he was crazy.

"What the hell you mean I'm going to have a big belly?" He leaned in and kissed me on my cheek.

"You're pregnant, Clay. I don't know why it's taking your ass so long to realize it." I knew Rome wanted me to have his baby, but I knew for a fact that I wasn't pregnant. I knew my body better than he did. My period comes on like clockwork, so the joke is on him. Or was it? It was way past time for my period to come on. Maybe it was just because I had been stressing a lot lately. Yep. That's exactly what it was. I ignored the look that Rome was giving me and dug into the food that was in front of me. I wasn't entertaining him right now. I wasn't having a baby anytime soon, so he could really get out of my face with this.

After I had eaten the wonderful breakfast that my man prepared for me, he took me upstairs and laid me down on the bed. He removed the night pants I was wearing, and I already knew what it was that he had in mind. He started from my feet and kissed all the way up until he reached my thighs. Spreading my legs apart, he slowly ran his tongue from the front to the back of my opening.

"Mmmm," I moaned. This was the best feeling in the world. He had me on the verge of cumming already and he had just started. He was moaning like he was the one getting pleasured. That only made me want it even more. He knew exactly what he was doing and it had me going crazy.

"Yess…Romee! I'm gonna cummm!" I yelled. As soon as I said it, I was releasing my juices all in his mouth. He made sure he caught every last drop. He looked up at me, then he started smiling.

"That's still my favorite meal," he said, getting up and walking into the bathroom.

"What are you doing? How are you just going to start something like this, then not finish it?" I asked, mad as hell. I wanted some dick and he was playing.

"Did you forget that I have a shop to run? Don't worry, I'll give you the dick as soon as I get off. Fucking around with you, I'm not going to make it in." I knew what he was saying was true, but I was still sitting there on the bed, pouting like a big ass three-year-old. I guess I would just see what Kaya was doing today. She and I hadn't talked in a while. I guess because I had been too busy with the drama going on in my life. I felt a little bad though. I didn't even know how my bestie was feeling. I picked up the phone and called her.

"Hey, best bitch, what you doing?" she answered.

"Nothing, just watching Rome get ready for work. You wanna come over and watch movies with me so I won't be lonely?"

"Of course. We need to talk anyway. I'll be over in about an hour," she let me know. I was happy as hell that she was coming over. I could really talk to her about any and everything.

"I'm about to leave. I'll call to check up on you later," Rome said, kissing me. I rolled my eyes at him. He always said that he would call and check up on me, but he never would. I would have to call and check up on him and most of the time, he wouldn't even answer the phone. He always claimed it got busy, but I didn't care; you answer the damn phone when I call.

Once he was gone, I took a quick shower and threw on some sweats because I was just going to be chilling in the house today. I put my hair up into a messy bun and made my way down the stairs. As soon as I got down there, there was a knock at the door. I didn't expect Kaya so soon. Maybe she sped over here or something.

Opening the door, I was surprised to see Erica standing there. She looked a downright mess. Her eye was swollen shut, she had a busted lip, and she had dried up blood coming from her nose. What the hell happened to her?

"Erica, what the hell happened? Who did this to you?" I asked, letting her into the house.

"My boyfriend. I told him that I was in love with Royal and he lost his mind. He even put me out of the house." I shook my head and led her to the bathroom so that I could help her clean her face up.

"Wait, you told your boyfriend you're in love with Royal? Kaya's boyfriend?" I asked. I didn't even know that she knew who Royal was.

"She doesn't deserve him! She is a fucking prostitute! And you know what else, my boyfriend called me her name during sex the other day. Before I even introduced them. I asked him about it today and he told me that he's been fucking her. He's been fucking her and giving her money. What kind of shit is that?"

"First of all, Erica, stop calling her a prostitute because she is far from it. I'm your friend and all, but I'll go to war over her, so watch your damn mouth." I didn't care that Erica was in her feelings right now. She wasn't about to sit here and talk about my best friend like she wasn't shit. That just wasn't going to happen.

"Why does everyone love her so much? She's ruined my life. Royal always told me that he doesn't do relationships, but here he is with that bitch," Erica continued.

"Because this bitch is the shit. It's not my fault your whack ass pussy and head game wasn't enough to make him wife you. It's crazy how you have a whole boyfriend but worried about mine. You really need to get your shit together," Kaya said, walking into the bathroom. Erica looked scared as hell that Kaya had heard her talking shit. I just shook my head because I couldn't stand a scary bitch. Don't talk shit if you can't back it up.

"You're a hoe, Kaya. Why are you proud of that?" Erica asked. Kaya just laughed. She wasn't even bothered by what Erica was saying.

"Why are you so pressed about me, girl? That's not a good look. Tell your nigga to stop blowing up my phone because it's starting to get really annoying." Kaya blew Erica a kiss and walked out of the bathroom. I wanted to laugh so bad, but I didn't.

"I can't stand her. She really thinks she's better than everyone." Erica was still going on about Kaya. She was really acting like a damn fan.

"Girl, shut the hell up. If she comes back in here and beats your ass, I'm not going to be able to help you out." Erica didn't say anything else after that. I was glad when I was done cleaning her face so I could go talk to my bestie. Erica went to go lay in my guest bedroom so she could rest. I knew it was only because Kaya was here. I didn't care though. She could stay in that guest bedroom. It didn't make me no difference.

"Okay, I'm done tending to her ass," I said, walking into the living room where Kaya was watching a movie.

"Good. Her desperate ass is annoying as hell. Why is she even over here?" Kaya asked with an obvious attitude. I knew she didn't really care for Erica like that, but now she was acting like she hated the girl. What the hell happened between them?

"She showed up with her face all bruised up. I asked her what happened and she told me that her boyfriend beat her because she told him that she was in love with Royal." Kaya started laughing like I had told a joke. Well, I guess it was a joke to her. I would probably laugh at some shit like that too.

"Girl, what? She came to our table yesterday trying to act like we were cool and shit. I knew she just wanted to be in Royal's face. She let him know that I was fucking niggas for money, now he's acting like he doesn't want anything to do with me. I should go up there and beat her ass, but I'm trying my hardest not to." I could tell that she was mad as hell. Who wouldn't be mad about something like that? I'd be ready to beat Erica's ass too.

"Damn, what did he say about it?" I asked, shocked that Erica had even gone that far.

"He hasn't really said much about it. Shit, he hasn't even talked to me today. I've called him and he hasn't answered not one of my calls." Kaya picked her phone up to look at the screen, but sat it right back down.

"He's acting like you were walking the streets fucking random ass niggas. You were fucking niggas that you know, then on top of all that, it was only two niggas that you were doing it with. He's really overreacting." Out of nowhere, Kaya started bawling like a baby. This was something that didn't happen very often. Kaya wasn't the type to let people know how she was feeling. She always kept her feelings bottled up until she exploded. I guess she was at her breaking point.

"Kaya, what's wrong?" I asked, hugging her. She told me everything from her being pregnant and losing the baby, all the way to her robbing Royal and not even knowing that it was his house. I didn't even know that she was going through all of this. I was starting to feel like I was a terrible friend because here my bestie was going through some shit and this is the first of me even hearing about it. Royal ignoring her wasn't making the situation better at all. I just hugged her until she stopped crying. I really wish that I could take all of her pain away, but I couldn't. I hated seeing her like this.

"Everything is going to be okay, I promise," I let her know.

"If he breaks up with me, I'm beating her ass," she sobbed into my chest. I didn't even say anything back. Erica would really deserve that ass whoopin'. I wouldn't even feel bad for her at all. I couldn't even imagine what Kaya was going through right now. Losing a baby is something that I never want to go through. The thought of losing a child made me sick to my stomach. I quickly got off the couch and ran into the bathroom, releasing all of the breakfast that I had eaten earlier. I hate throwing up. This shit was the worse.

"Bitch, you pregnant?" Kaya asked, standing at the door. Her eyes were red and puffy as hell from all the crying she had just done.

"No, I'm not pregnant," I said, trying to convince myself.

"You sure? When is your period supposed to be on?"

"Now. I'm just stressed out right now, that's why it hasn't come yet." Kaya chuckled.

"Do you even believe the bullshit that just came out of your mouth?"

"It's not bullshit, and yes, I believe it," I said, getting up so that I could rinse my mouth out. Kaya just stood there giving me a knowing look, so I didn't look at her. I walked right past her like I didn't see her.

"Damn, Clay. Go take a pregnancy test. I know you got some here," she finally said. I guess she was tired of me acting like this wasn't a big deal. She was right though. I did have pregnancy tests here for emergencies. After the first pregnancy scare that I had, I made sure to keep them in the house.

"I don't need to take a test, Kaya."

"I will drag you up the stairs and make you take that test. Don't play with me." I sighed and got off the couch. The only reason I did was because I knew that Kaya was telling the truth. She was strong as hell and she could probably throw my little ass over her shoulder if she really wanted to.

Once I got upstairs in the bathroom, I pulled out the box of pregnancy tests and just stared at them. I didn't want to do this at all, but I took a deep breath and opened the pack. Two came in one box, so I made sure I had enough piss for both of them.

"What's taking so long? I'm tired of waiting," Kaya said, scaring the shit out of me.

"Bitch, don't be sneaking up on me like that. You almost gave me a damn heart attack," I said, clutching my chest. She rolled her eyes and came into the bathroom with me.

"How many minutes are you supposed to wait?"

"Three, why?"

"Well, how many minutes has it been?"

"I literally just sat them down. I didn't even have time to wash my hands yet because you wanted to barge in here scaring people and shit," I said, rolling my eyes.

"Well, they both say positive," she let me know. I heard what she said, but for some reason, it didn't register. I couldn't be pregnant. The tests had to be broken or something. Maybe they were old. I felt like I was in a bad dream right now.

"Are you sure?" was the only thing I could think of to say.

"Uhh, yeah, I'm sure. I can read perfectly fine. Your ass is knocked up." She started smiling, and I didn't know how to feel. My chest felt like it was going to cave in. I wasn't ready to be a mom. I could barely take care of myself. I don't even want to think about what my mom is going to have to say. She's going to bring up the fact that Rome and I aren't married. I started to shake my head.

"This cannot be happening," I said to myself.

"Girl, why the hell you trippin'? It's not like you have a job or anything. Rome takes perfect care of you, so what makes you think he's not going to do the same for the baby?" Kaya asked, following me into the bedroom. I loved how she put her problems aside for mine. She was a real friend for that.

"That's not what I'm worried about, Kay. We still aren't married. What if he just wakes up one day and decides that he doesn't want to be with me anymore? Then what? I don't want to be a single mother. What if I turn out to be a bad mom? Shit, what if I turn out like my mom?" I loved my mom to death, but she could've done better as a mom I feel. It's like after she left my dad, she changed for the worse and not better. It was kind of sad. She hasn't even dated since she left him, and that was years ago.

That's something that I don't want to happen. I didn't want to lose myself in a man. I felt like it was too late for that though. I loved Rome with everything in me, so if he left me, I wouldn't know how to act. I would probably just shut down, and if I have a baby, that's not going to be good at all.

"You know Rome worships the ground you walk on. He's not going anywhere. You need to stop worrying about the irrelevant shit and be happy that you have a man that actually wants to start a family. Some of these bitches get pregnant and the nigga dips out. Stop thinking about all the negatives. You are lucky girl." I guess she was right about that. That's not the only thing I was worried about though.

"What if he cheats on me again?" I think that was the main reason I didn't want to have a baby. If he cheated again, I would not take him back. He only got one time with cheating on me, and sometimes I feel like I shouldn't have taken him back this time.

"If he cheats on you again, then you cut his dick off. Plain and simple." I looked at Kaya and waited to see if she was going to start laughing, but she didn't. Her face was so damn serious. I couldn't help but laugh at her. She was crazy as hell. I didn't think Royal knew who he was fucking with.

"So if Royal cheated on you, you're cutting his dick off?" I asked, just to be sure.

"Hell yeah, and I'm killing whoever the bitch is. He better hope I don't catch them two together because it's going to be lights out for both of them. I will be in jail that day, and when I'm sitting in that jail cell, I'm not even going to be mad at myself. I hate how niggas think they can just play with our emotions like that. Cheating is probably the worst thing you can ever do to a woman. I don't care what anyone says." I agreed with everything she was saying. I remember feeling so low after Rome cheated on me. Then on top of it all, I caught him in the act. That's enough to make any bitch go crazy.

"I just don't trust him anymore. It's like every time I turn around, it's some drama about some bitch. Lately, it's just been her. I think she finally got the hint though. She hasn't been a problem for us or anything."

"Good. You just need to make sure it stays that way. You know I have no problem killing a bitch." Kaya was crazy. I never realized how crazy she was until we had this conversation that we're having right now. I was glad that I had her as my best friend though, because I might be needing her soon. For some reason, I just didn't feel like we had seen the last of this Nikki bitch. If she wanted to try me again, I might have to get Kaya to end her life.

# Chapter Twenty-One: Nikki

I had been calling Rome nonstop and all of my calls went unanswered. I knew his little girlfriend had everything to do with why he was ignoring me. Rome should know better by now. You don't ignore Nikki. That's when I start to act up. I didn't care about his relationship with that girl. If you ask me, he deserved way better anyway. He needs to be with someone like me, and not her wannabe thug ass.

I had been following Rome around lately. For some reason, I wanted to know where he was at all times. I just needed to be close to him again. I thought about popping up at his place of work again, but I didn't want to risk running into his girlfriend and getting my ass beat again. Yeah, I wanted Rome bad as hell, but I didn't want to keep getting beat up. I thought there was going to be permanent damage to my face after she finished with me, but there wasn't. I was so thankful that I had my beautiful face back.

I sat outside of Rome's house wondering what he was in there doing. This was the house that we made love in. I still remember that day like it was yesterday. I just wish he would stop ignoring me so that we could have another one of those days. I know he wants me just as bad as I want him. He's just putting on a front right now.

I called his phone and it rang two times before it went straight to voicemail. He saw me calling, he was just ignoring my calls. I didn't understand why he was doing that. He was home alone because I watched Clay leave. He kissed her ass like she wasn't coming back or something. I really wished that she wasn't.

The front door swung open and out walked some female that I had never seen before. Damn, it looks like he was still cheating on Clay. Poor dumb girl. She didn't even know that her nigga wanted everyone except her.

Looking at the girl, I got mad as hell. She wasn't even cute. She was so skinny, she looked like a damn crackhead. He wouldn't fuck with me anymore, but he was fucking with the help? That's exactly what she looked like to me. I shook my head and called his phone again. To my surprise, he actually answered this time.

"Stop fucking calling my phone, Nikki! Why can't you take the hint that I don't want anything to do with you?!" he yelled into the phone. This was not the answer that I was expecting, but at least he answered.

"Rome, why are you treating me like this? You want me just as much as I want you. I'm getting wet just thinking about all of the things you were doing to my body."

"I have a girl. I'm not fucking with you like that ever again. What's so hard to understand about that? If my girl finds out that you're still calling my phone, that's gonna be your ass, and this time, I'm not going to be able to save you."

I didn't like how he was talking. All he cared about was his stupid girlfriend and her feelings. What about me and my feelings? He didn't give a fuck about those.

"What's so good about her? Why won't you just let me be your side hoe? I know how to stay in my place. I promise." Rome started laughing and I didn't know what the hell he thought was so funny. I was serious as hell. I didn't mind being his side hoe at all.

"That right there is why she's better than you. A woman should never want to be a side hoe. Have some damn respect for yourself. My girl would never say some dumb shit like that. Just leave me the fuck alone, Nikki. I'm not gonna say it no more."

"But Rome—" I started to say, but he hung up the phone. To say my feelings were hurt would be an understatement. He had me so fucked up if he thought that I was just going to give up that easily. I needed him. I needed him more than I needed air to breathe. He had that effect on me and I didn't understand why. I needed to find a way to get him back. I didn't know what I was going to do, but something had to happen.

I sat outside of his house for a couple more minutes before I finally decided to start my car and head home. I hate living alone. It was lonely as hell and that's when I started thinking about Rome the most. Everything about him was just so perfect. I would get wet just thinking about him and his big fat dick. He had the type of dick that would have a bitch going crazy.

When I was finally home in my bed, I pulled out my phone and started scrolling through Rome's Facebook. This was something that I did every day. He didn't really post much, but his little girlfriend Clay did. She was always uploading pictures of them two and tagging him in them. The other day she uploaded a picture of the breakfast that he had cooked for her. She was really annoying. That should be me that he's cooking for, not her! She doesn't even deserve him!

Scrolling down Rome's page, I didn't see anything other than that bitch tagging him in pictures and statuses saying how much she loved him. I couldn't help but roll my eyes at everything she posted. I stopped scrolling when I came across a status that Rome had posted that read: *Looks like I'm going to be a dad.* I reread the status at least fifty times before I sat the phone down. This could not be happening. He really got this bitch pregnant? Now he would never leave her ass! It should be me that's carrying his baby! Why was he so pressed over her? I didn't understand it. The tears started falling and I felt sick to my stomach. I knew I shouldn't have gotten that abortion after he and I had sex. Things would be so different now. Maybe he and I would even be together right now, but I had to go and get rid of the baby like a dumb ass.

I didn't know what to do, so I picked up the phone to call Reese. She always gave the best advice.

"Hello?" she said sleepily into the phone.

"Reese, he got that bitch pregnant!" I cried into the phone.

"Girl, what are you talking about? Who's pregnant?"

"Rome got his stupid little girlfriend pregnant. That should be me carrying his baby. Not her. Why is he doing this to me? He even hung up on me earlier. Why is he treating me like this?"

"Oh my gosh. Nikki, you need to leave that man alone and let him live his life. He got that girl pregnant because they are actually in a relationship. What you two once had is over. You need to let all of that go," she had the nerve to say. What the hell? This was not the advice I was expecting.

"I love him, Reese," I said.

"How?! How can you love a man that only fucked you once? How can you love a man that keeps telling you that he doesn't want to lose his girlfriend so he wants nothing to do with you? How can you love a man that you almost got killed over? Let it go, Nikki. Let him go and find you someone that is actually willing to love you back." Everything she was saying wasn't doing anything but making me even more upset than I already was. I couldn't believe her right now. She was supposed to be on my side, not his.

"You wouldn't understand because you never got fucked by a black man. You're so used to those little dick ass white boys so of course, you don't know how I'm feeling," I bitterly said. Reese started laughing.

"Bitch, for your information, I have had sex with a black man. In fact, I'm laying right beside my black man. Oh, and you know what else? I know for a fact that my black man is mine and mine only. Can you say the same about yours? Oh wait, you can't because you don't have a man. You're too busy trying to steal someone else's man and he doesn't even want you." I could tell from the tone of her voice that I had pissed her off. I didn't care, though. She was supposed to be on my side and she wasn't.

"Fuck you, Reese!" I yelled, then hung up the phone. Fuck that bitch. She was supposed to help me come up with a plan to get rid of Clay, but instead, she wanted to tell me to leave him alone. Why would I do some crazy shit like that? Why would I give up on the person that I love and that I'm in love with? So what we only had sex one time. That was the best sex that I had ever had in my life. Fuck what Reese was talking about.

I guess I was just going to have to do this myself since Reese wouldn't help me. I was perfectly capable of doing things by myself. I didn't need her for shit. Some friend she was. If she were in the situation that I'm in, I would jump at the opportunity to help her get rid of a bitch. I would help with whatever it was that she needed help with. I guess her loyalty didn't run as deep as mine did. That's what I get for being loyal to the wrong damn people. I wiped the tears that had fallen down my cheeks and laid down in my bed. I had something planned for Clay tomorrow, and the best part about it was she didn't suspect a thing.

The next morning, I woke up and quickly got out of bed. I had important shit to do today, so I made sure to take a quick shower. I didn't have time to get all dressed up and cute. I threw on a pair of sweatpants and a tank top. I made sure to wear some old tennis shoes too. I put my hair in a low ponytail and I was out the door. I drove straight to Rome's house and parked across the street so they wouldn't see me. I knew Rome was probably at work because his car wasn't in the driveway. His stupid girlfriend's was, though. I took a deep breath because I didn't know how this was going to turn out, then I got out of the car.

Making sure I had my pepper spray in my pocket, I slowly made my way to their front door. I didn't really think this whole thing through. I was running off of emotions. The closer I got to their front door, the more nervous I got. There was no turning back now. I banged on the door like I was the police. They didn't have a peephole or anything, so she would have to answer the door to see who it was.

"Who the fuck is banging on my door like that?!" I heard her stupid ass yell before she snatched the door open. I didn't even give her a chance to really see me before I sprayed my pepper spray in her face. She screamed and fell to the ground. That's when I started beating her ass like she did me that night at the tattoo shop, and boy did it feel good. I was punching the shit out of her when I remembered that she was pregnant. I tried to kick her in her stomach, but she curled up into a ball and was holding her stomach with her hands. Stupid bitch.

"Rome is my man, bitch!" I yelled, kicking her in her back. "You need to leave him the fuck alone!" Next thing I knew, I had been hit over the head with something heavy and I fell to the ground. My vision was blurry and I couldn't see who it was standing over me, but I could still see a figure. After that, everything went black.

# Chapter Twenty-Two: Royal

After what Kaya had told me the other day at dinner, I hadn't really been talking to her like that. She called my phone day and night, but I just couldn't bring myself to answer it. Yeah, I know that the shit happened before she and I had even gotten together, but I still couldn't bring myself to talk to her. I felt like she should have better morals than that. I didn't want to fuck with her like that anymore. I guess you could say that I was a single man now.

I guess it was a little fucked up that I didn't tell Kaya how I was feeling, but I just couldn't bring myself to talk to her. I already had a problem because she was stripping every night, but finding out that she was basically a prostitute made shit ten times worse. No man wants to find out that their girl was fucking niggas for money. That was some low shit to do. I don't care how bad you're struggling.

"Are you coming back to bed, Daddy?" I heard Roxy ask from behind me. I had been fucking her for the past couple of days because it was easy pussy. She would throw herself at me every time I came to the strip club anyway, so I just figured why not? The only thing was, her pussy couldn't even compare to Kaya's and it was annoying as hell. It seemed like I was always comparing Roxy to Kaya. Roxy wasn't even cute outside of the club. That makeup worked wonders for her. The only thing Roxy really had was ass and titties. She could suck a mean dick though. That was probably the reason I had this hoe all up and through my house that I planned to share with Kaya.

"Yeah, I'll be there in a minute," I told her. I was standing outside on the balcony, smoking a blunt. I felt my phone vibrating in my pocket and I already knew that it was Kaya either calling or texting me. I was thinking about just blocking her number, but I couldn't bring myself to do that. I still had feelings for her, we just needed a break right now. It's what's best for us.

Walking back into the bedroom, Roxy was laid out on the bed, naked as the day she was born. I don't know what was going on with me right now, but I just wasn't in the mood to fuck her. I really just wanted to take my ass to sleep.

"Well, are you gonna just stand there and drool over me, or are you gonna fuck me?" she asked, licking her chapped ass lips. That was another turn off about Roxy. Her lips were always dehydrated as fuck. They were chapped to the point that they were cracking. She didn't even look good while sucking my dick because he lips looked so damn bad.

"Nah, I'm good. I'm chillin' right now," I said, sitting on the edge of the bed.

"Why? We've been fucking for like two days straight."

"Exactly, so you should be good."

"Well, will you at least come watch me at the club tonight?" I looked at that bitch like she was crazy. Why the hell would I take my ass down to that club knowing Kaya works there too? I knew she was just trying to be messy.

"Nah, you know damn well that ain't about to happen, bruh," I said, getting pissed off with this conversation.

"Why not? You scared you're gonna run into your little girlfriend?" She was smirking at me and I wanted to slap that shit right off of her face.

"Why would I be afraid to run into her? I'm a grown ass man."

"Then bring your grown ass to the club then."

"Not about to happen. Go make your money and find a way back here tonight," I said, kicking my shoes off and getting comfortable on the bed. She just stared at me like she was shocked or some shit. I didn't care though. She wasn't my bitch. She better be lucky I even had her in my damn house.

"You're an asshole, Royal."

"But you were basically begging to fuck me," I chuckled.

"Boy bye, I only fucked you because Kaya told me to stay away from you. I had to let her know that I do what I want and that I can fuck whoever I want. Don't nobody run me." All this talk about Kaya was starting to make me feel bad. For the first time since I dropped her off at her crib, I was actually starting to miss her. I was so messed up for doing her like this without even talking to her first.

"Then get the hell out. You're no longer needed." She looked as if she wanted to break down and start crying right here. I just shook my head and laughed at her. She was trying to put on a front like she didn't want a nigga, but we all knew that was a lie. My phone started ringing in my pocket again and I pulled it out, only to see that it was Rome calling.

"What's good?" I asked.

"Man, get to the hospital right now, bruh," he said. My thoughts instantly went to Kaya. Had something happened to her? Was she okay? Was she calling earlier because she needed my help?

"What's going on?" I asked, not sure if I was ready to hear the answer.

"It's Clay. I'll tell you once you get here." He ended the call and I quickly got off the bed.

"Aye girl, it's time for you to go. I'll hit you up later though," I said, putting my shoes back on and looking for a shirt.

"What? Why?"

"Don't fucking question me. Just do what the fuck I said, and hurry up." She was moving way too slow for me. I was about to throw her ass out naked and not even give a fuck. She finally started to put her clothes on but she was still moving too slow for me.

"Hurry the fuck up! Damn, why you going all slow and shit. I got important shit to handle right now," I snapped. She looked up at me like she wanted to say something, but she quickly decided against it. Kaya would be cussing my ass out right now if I would've said something like that to her. That's why I couldn't fuck with these regular ass bitches—they had no backbone.

Once I got Roxy out of my house, I was in the car and on the way to the hospital. I was praying that everything was good with Clay. I didn't want my boy to have a mental breakdown or some shit. He was about to lose his mind when she left his ass. I could only imagine how he would react if something happened to her.

I spotted Rome in the waiting room as soon as I walked in. He looked like he was really stressing. Erica was sitting right beside him. I didn't know why she was here, but I was hoping like hell Rome wasn't fucking her.

"What happened?" I asked, sitting down beside Rome.

"Nikki came to the house and attacked Clay." I just looked at his ass. I knew he should've moved after he stopped fucking with that bitch. She shouldn't have even been in his house. Now she knows where he lives and she's attacking people and shit.

"What? Where the hell were you at when all of this shit was going down?" I asked.

"I had just left for work. Erica was the one who got Nikki off of her. She hit her in the head with a metal bat." Erica looked at me and smiled. I wasn't fucking with that bitch no more, though. She was the real reason I wasn't fucking with Kaya right now. If she would've just kept her mouth shut and wouldn't have even come to our table, I wouldn't know what I know and Kaya and I would still be good.

"She's pregnant," Rome said. Damn. All this nigga ever wanted was to start a family with Clay. I know he's going to try to kill Nikki if Clay loses this baby.

"Is the baby good?"

"Shit, I don't know yet. I don't know shit. They won't tell me anything. Erica said that Nikki was really just kicking her in her back, though. I swear if I lose my child because of this bitch, I'm killing her ass. Nah, I'm killing her ass anyway. She took shit way too far." I agreed with Rome one hundred percent. If some shit like that ever happened to Kaya, I'd probably cut the bitch's head off. You don't mess with someone's wife like that.

I found myself sitting here thinking about Kaya. She was everything that I wanted in a woman. I had never felt like this before, and here I am ignoring her ass over some shit that happened in her past. I wasn't shit and I knew it. She probably didn't want shit to do with me now. It's been a little minute since my phone rang. She must've got tired of me ignoring her. I decided that I was going to make everything up to her tomorrow. I just hoped that she would be willing to give my ass another chance.

# Chapter Twenty-Three: Kaya

I was so tired of Royal ignoring me. I called and texted him nonstop and I didn't get not one answer. He didn't even have a real reason as to why he wasn't talking to me. He was really mad over something that happened before he and I had even gotten together. He can't be mad at something that happened in the past. Shit, we've all got a past. His was probably worse than mine anyway.

I thought about popping up at his house and showing out. I was going to bust all of the windows out of his car, then I was going to go inside and fuck everything up in there too. Who did he think he was? Ignoring me like I'm just some random bitch and not his damn girlfriend! I decided against that, though. What would that solve? Not a damn thing.

I actually decided that I was going to go to his house early in the morning and cook him breakfast. He and I could talk like two adults over breakfast. I wasn't going to yell, cuss, or swing at him. I actually wanted to have a real conversation and figure out why he wasn't fucking with me.

Shit like this never happened. I was never blowing up someone's phone. I never double texted someone. I damn sure didn't lurk on a nigga's social media just to see what he was doing and if he was parading around another bitch. Royal really had me acting like I was one of these desperate ass bitches that was begging for his attention. That's not how shit worked in my world, though. He was going to talk to me whether he wanted to or not.

I made sure to wake up bright and early. I got in the shower, straightened my hair, and threw on a nice yellow sundress that had my ass looking right. Knowing Royal, he would probably be ready to fuck when he lays his eyes on me. That was my plan, though. I wanted him to see what it was that he was missing out on.

After making sure that I looked good enough to eat, I got in my car and made my way to Royal's house. I didn't have a key or anything, but I was a master at picking locks. It wouldn't be hard for me to get in at all. I was just hoping that he had gone grocery shopping because if he hadn't, that was going to throw off my whole plan. I was starving too.

I got out of my car and made my way to the front door. After picking the lock, I was in his house with ease. It was still early, so I knew his ass was probably still knocked out. Most of the time he didn't wake up until the afternoon anyway.

I slipped my shoes off and quietly made my way up the stairs to his room. I just wanted to peek at him and see him sleeping. It had been a couple of days since I saw his face and I was missing him terribly. I hated that he was acting so childish. I wouldn't even have to go through all of this if he would've let me explain my life to him. He didn't want to do that, though. He just wanted to act like a little bitch because I was getting money after sex. Well, when I say it like that, it sounds bad as hell.

Peeking my head into Royal's room, I got the shock of a lifetime. Royal was laid out on the bed, naked as hell, and beside him was Roxy's hoe ass. I see that she didn't take heed to my warning. That alone had me wanting to hit her, but at the same time, I didn't want to wake them up. They looked so peaceful sleeping. It was disgusting. I just stood there in the doorway, watching them sleep. I see that Royal didn't miss me at all for the past couple of days.

I wanted to break down and start crying, but I didn't. Instead, I quietly went down the stairs and into the kitchen. I got the sharpest knife that I could find and went back upstairs into their room.

Before Roxy knew what was happening, I took the knife and slit her throat. Watching her struggle to breathe and choke on her own blood was making me happy. I was feeling a little better, but not much. I don't like it when people underestimate me. If I wanted to, I could kill Royal's ass too, but I know I would be the main one at the funeral crying. Plus, I wanted him to see what I had done.

I watched as Roxy choked and struggled until she went silent and her body wasn't moving anymore. I couldn't believe this shit. Out of all the girls he could've cheated on me with, he really chose this raggedy ass hoe? She knew exactly what she was doing too. She only went after Royal because I told her to leave him alone. She should've listened to me, though. She would've still been alive today.

Right when I was about to turn to leave, a brilliant idea popped into my head. I dipped my finger in the blood that had squirted from Roxy's neck and wrote big as hell on his wall:

KAYA WAS HERE

I couldn't wait for him to wake up and see it. He really cheated on the wrong one. It was okay, though. He was going to learn the hard way that I am not to be fucked with.

**To Be Continued...**

CPSIA information can be obtained
at www.ICGtesting.com
Printed in the USA
LVOW10s0037280217
525566LV00016B/206/P